Stupid Cupid

Stupid Cupid

Ankit Sonthalia

Srishti
PUBLISHERS & DISTRIBUTORS

Srishti Publishers & Distributors
Registered Office: N-16, C.R. Park
New Delhi – 110 019
Corporate Office: 212A, Peacock Lane
Shahpur Jat, New Delhi – 110 049
editorial@srishtipublishers.com

First published by
Srishti Publishers & Distributors in 2016

To my lovely mom, whom I miss every day,
To my caring dad,
To my funny sister,
To my dashing father-in-law,
To my innocent mother-in-law,
To my beautiful sister-in-law,
And to the rest of my supportive family.

Acknowledgements

No good work is ever complete without the support one gets from the people around him. I would like to thank the following people for making this novel possible.

Ankita, who happened to be my girlfriend once, for giving me inspiration to describe all the pretty ladies in the book. Though none of my words can do justice to her beauty.

My best friend Ankita, for boosting me up whenever I was on the verge of giving up. (It happened quite a few times).

My personal critic Ankita, for giving my manuscript the honest suggestions it needed so that I could at least think about getting it published in the first place.

And finally, my lovely wife Ankita, the reason behind my even thinking of writing a novel.

I look forward to my readers' feedback on the story with bated breath. Please do send in your feedback and suggestions to ankitsonthalia1@gmail.com.

Prologue

I got out of my car and stood at the gate of Namgyal Monastery in Dharamsala, one of the largest Buddhist monasteries in the country.

"Hey, isn't that Suhaan?"

"Yes, and that's his BMW. I saw him getting into it yesterday outside the hotel."

"Of course it's him. Who else can manage to look so sexy in a plain white shirt and blue denims?" a group of girls were chatting near me where I could hear them.

"Oh my god! He looks even better in reality than on the screen!" The next moment they rushed towards me and requested to click a few pictures.

I had read a story about Mr Sachin Tendulkar obliging his fans for pictures and autographs once at one in the morning. It said he'd never let his fans down in this matter and so, being a huge fan of his, I did the same even when I was in no mood for it.

All kinds of pictures were taken – selfies, groupies, couple photographs. A couple of them hugged me tightly enough to make sure absolutely nothing could pass between us – not even air.

"Where can I meet His Holiness?" I asked a monk entering the gate.

"He must be in his chamber or in the garden, but you can't meet him like this," he said continuing to walk inside while I followed him.

"But he knows me. In fact, he has invited me here," I said.

"I get a lot of fanatics who tell me this every day. I can't let everyone meet him," he said.

"May I know who you are, by the way?"

"I am the head of the Gaden Phodrang, which means the Office of His Holiness," he replied.

"Great! Could you please just at least let him know I am here and let him decide if he wants to meet me or not?" I pleaded. He finally agreed.

"Your Holiness, allow me to introduce mys..." I said when I got a chance to meet His Holiness after hours of waiting.

"I remember you, son. I remember very well that we met at the stadium, and somehow I had the feeling we would meet again someday," he said interrupting me.

"Yes, Your Holiness, you asked me to meet you if I had anything to talk about, and here I am to unload my burden."

"Tell me son, what is it?" he asked.

I got into NRMC University near Ahmedabad. It is one of the most prestigious colleges in the country, and with the kind of academic background I had, I couldn't have asked for more. I had been nothing but an average student during my school days and had somehow worked nights to get good grades and get into NRMC, not before the incessant pestering by my father. I was there to study Business Management. Until then, I was just following the path of life, wherever it decided to take me. I always maintained that I wanted to explore different things and do whatever interests me, but one thing which I was sure about was that I wanted to get famous. Whenever my father would ask me about my future plans, I'd always say, "I want to live the best life of all."

My family is into coal chemicals and also dealt in real estate at times. Hence we had more money than one needed to live a comfortable life. Dad had forced me into joining this college as he wanted me to have a good education if in case I couldn't pursue my dreams. My parents had always been a pillar of support for me. They knew they had a reputed name in the society and there wasn't the need for me to go for an unconventional career option. They, however, always considered my dreams as theirs.

NRMC boasted of a huge campus. The campus gates itself gave a picture of what one could expect inside. It had huge steel gates which were akin to a palace's entrance. There was a security cabin to the right with at least two guards on duty at all times who would keep a check of everything from a pin to a trailer going in.

The university was sprawled over eighteen hundred acres. It was one of a kind in the entire country. It offered more courses than any other college did. Engineering, medical, arts, literature, architecture, law – you name it and they had it. They had the best staff possible because most of them were picked up from the colleges which were best in their respective courses. It was more of a mini-city than a college. The campus had everything that one could imagine. There were huge hostel buildings with two hundred rooms in each, with one room accommodating two students. The stupendous dining hall served five thousand students daily; their Olympic size swimming pools, a football and a cricket ground which conducted intra and inter college matches; volleyball, basketball, badminton courts; a horse race course, and almost all other sports which exist.

The library boasted of thousands of volumes. It was a seven-storey building and had the reputation of being one of the biggest in the country. There were two huge auditoriums and an open amphitheatre which witnessed many seminars, lectures, plays besides other activities round the year. There were four big college cafeterias which served all the local snacks, apart from the two huge CCD outlets where you could hardly get an empty seat. One could think of them as chick magnets. The boys could spot all types of girls they ever dreamt of – from all over the country and even abroad. Short and cute ones, tall ones with long, perfectly-shaped legs, the ones with ample bosoms, the ones with low neck line tops, and also the tom-boyish ones. That was the place where a new girl could sit for twenty minutes in a sexy skirt and a tube top and become well-known around the college in the next twenty.

I got down from my car at the administrative building and looked around the wide expanse of the enormity of my college to be. Obviously, I couldn't see the boundaries of the campus. I had insisted that my parents do not come; I thought it was too childish and had requested only for the driver. As I entered the building, I could see a few other students filling up forms and walking from one counter to the other where the admission process was going on. After completing the formalities, I was given directions to my room. It took me a while, but I finally managed to reach my room. It was on the third floor in C.P.S House. It was a six-storey building, very similar to the administrative building. It was a single, interconnected C-shaped building. The middle portion was open to the sky and had a volleyball court for the students. There were a few hostel buildings in the campus for different courses and each building was named after one of the founder members. C.P.S. stood for Chandubhai Popatlal Shah. The floors were huge with long corridors and my room was at the end one corridor. It was a long walk to my room.

"Oh man!" I exclaimed as soon as I used the key to enter the room.

I had been in a hostel before, with boys with the weirdest of habits, and had been caught in the most awkward of situations, but this was something else. There he was, Ramaraju Sambhashivam. Sprawled on his bed with his laptop facing the door, his hand was in his pants. He had his earphones on and was watching soft porn. It had only been a few hours since he had landed on the campus! I slammed the door and rushed out.

A few seconds later, Ramaraju opened the door, now looking decent.

"Err, you must be Suhaan Arora?" he asked hesitantly looking at me.

"Unfortunately, yes," I replied, still not looking at him.

"I am Ramaraju Sambhashivam, your roommate. I saw your name on the list while reporting."

He put forward his hand for a handshake.

"Namaste, glad to meet you," I said sarcastically turning towards him and joining my hands to greet him to avoid any physical contact whatsoever.

The difference in our physical attributes was something noteworthy. He was a short timid guy at five feet three inches. He was very thin, with round geek-like spectacles, wearing a local tailored pair of trousers and a white shirt with grey checks. I, on the other hand was five feet ten and fair complexioned. Thanks to my love for sports, I had a well-toned body. Raju and I looked like David and Goliath together. He also had a permanent two-day beard which never seemed to grow any longer, and neither did Ramaraju care to shave it.

Raju originally hailed from Vellore, Tamil Nadu, about a hundred and fifty kilometers from Chennai, famous for its educational institutes. His family had recently shifted to Vadodara due to his father's job, and luckily for them, Raju had also got into NRMC. His parents were happy that Raju would be able to visit them on weekends and holidays. The real reason why his parents wanted him close to them was that they wanted to keep an eye on him, which had become necessary after a certain incident.

"Err, please come in." Raju said as he led me back into the room.

After what I had seen, I wasn't too happy about going back as erasing that sight from my mind would take a long time. A very long time.

In the rectangular room, one of the shorter sides possessed the door where I was standing and there was a window on the opposite wall. Apart from this, it had two cupboards placed in diagonal corners and two single-beds adjoining the longer sides.

"I am sorry for what happened. I thought you'd be reporting late in the evening and I had the room to myself till then," Raju explained.

"Yeah whatever. Can't undo it now anyway." I smirked.

He was smiling sheepishly. "How come I am seeing a South Indian fellow in Gujarati land? They didn't accept you because of your desperation, eh?" I took a dig at him.

"My dad was transferred to Ahmedabad after twenty years of service with his company in Vellore. They are setting up a new unit and they needed someone experienced, and my parents wanted me to stay close to them. They didn't even want me to stay on campus, but I managed to convince them after a lot of persuasion."

"I can see why they wanted their little baby close to them. They wouldn't have wanted the king of Hornyville roaming around with his hand in his pants."

"Oh come on, man! I am already embarrassed after what happened. Stop it now. It's just one incident which got them worried."

"Yeah? I am all ears, bro."

"Well, it was one summer holiday when I was home and my mom had decided to visit her childhood friend in Bangalore for a few days. My dad couldn't join us because of work. Mom's friend, Tamanna aunty had come to pick us up at the railway station. She was divorced a couple of years ago and her only son lived in a hostel in Mumbai. So, she lived alone. I was about thirteen at that time and the moment I saw her, I realized what it meant when my older cousins had told me about puberty. Draped in a yellow sari and a sleeveless green blouse, there she was, walking towards us – tall, fair with long hair going down till just above her delicate waist. Her bosom was just perfect. Not that I had paid attention at that age, but still it felt they had an awesomeness about them."

I stopped him to get a glass of water and then asked him to continue.

"I couldn't get my eyes off her even for a moment. I still remember what pleasure it was when she herself took me in her arms, my face pressed against her bosoms as she greeted me.

The next few days seemed like paradise. I had never felt like that before. I wouldn't miss a glance at her visible cleavage, her waistline, or her butt. On the third day, I had lost count of how many times I had thanked my mother for bringing me along. And then it was doomsday. She was going to take a bath at nine in the morning like every day. The flat had two bathrooms sharing the same wall. The walls were high but at the top of it were a few flower shaped holes for ventilation."

"I can see where this is going. Please continue." I chuckled.

"I went into the other bathroom and climbed to the top taking the support of two buckets which rested on a small, albeit rickety stool. After some hard work, I had finally managed to get a good view. She entered the bathroom in her white robe and locked the door. The door was exactly opposite to the wall from which I was peeking. Just next to the door was a wash basin with a mirror above it. She hung a towel on the hook behind the door and went to the basin to brush her teeth. I was losing my patience with each passing second. She bent to rinse her mouth after checking her teeth in the mirror. Suddenly, I realized I could be visible in the mirror and ducked immediately. Finally, she removed the robe and what I saw next could be called the most wonderful sight of my life. She was standing there in a black bra and panty. She walked towards the shower which was on the adjacent wall towards my right and turned it on. Then, she unhooked her bra and removed it. The two most beautiful things in the world were right in front of my eyes. I gasped. The hard-on I had was unbelievable. And then she raised her hand to hang the bra on a hook on the wall from the top of which I was peeping.

"She shouted in fear, shock and anger while covering her assets when she spotted me.

"I was experiencing the same feeling, minus the anger, of course. I lost my balance as I moved away from the wall to hide, but it was too late. She had seen me. To top it, the buckets toppled over. I fell on the floor with a loud noise. All of a sudden, the heaven I was in vanished and hell appeared out of nowhere. What next? My mother, father, uncle, aunt, everyone in the society where I lived came to know about it. I was lucky it wasn't in the newspapers. I was given lectures, and a few sessions of counseling and was sentenced to house arrest for life. So that's the reason I'm here in NRMC instead of some college in South India."

"Fuck! You are one horny bastard man. I'll have to be careful and keep my pants on all the time around you," I exclaimed laughing.

And then we began talking and sharing things about our lives until it was time to hit the bed.

I have always been a fitness freak. Right from my school days, I would exercise regularly and play cricket at least four times a week. I had also been the school cricket team captain. I wanted to continue this habit and went for a little jog before getting ready on the first day in college.

Raju and I got ready in time and left for the classes. As soon as I entered the college building, I realized life was going to be something else. Apart from a few hot girls, I seemed to be the head turner for the day. I spotted at least a dozen girls checking me out and passing smiles. I was enjoying all the adulation as it was new for me. I had done my schooling from The Doon School in Dehradun, which wasn't a co-ed. This continued all day long – in the classroom, the cafeteria, the corridor during breaks, and so on.

Raju and I made a few more friends as the day passed by. I particularly enjoyed the company of Saurabh Singh and Akshay Singhal. They were ardent cricket fans. While Saurabh was a good cricketer himself, Akshay was more interested in sitting in the stands, not that his hundred and twenty kilogram body would have supported him even if he wanted to play. We went about in a normal routine for the next few days and I, Ramaraju, Saurabh and Akshay got friendlier with each other as time passed. We would attend the college in the morning and hang out in the cafeterias and our rooms till late at night.

After about a month, a third year student entered our classroom and made an announcement. "We are going to select our team for the intra-university cricket tournament from tomorrow onwards. Those who are interested, please give me your names," he said.

I, Saurabh and a few others immediately raised our hands.

"Good to see that so many freshers are interested. See you at the ground in front of the S.M.B (Sanjaybhai Mafatlal Bonny) hostel building tomorrow at seven in the morning sharp. Don't care to enter the ground if you are late even by a minute," he said and stormed off.

"Woah! Some attitude that guy has," I exclaimed.

"He's earned it, bro. He's Abhishek Gandhi, the BMS' and college university team's captain. We have always performed well in the intra-university tournaments since it started seven years ago, winning it twice and being in the finals on two more occasions. Abhishek is dying to win this year as he has been awarded the captaincy. He's a nice guy though. Just a little strict when it comes to the game."

The next morning, Saurabh and I reached the ground fifteen minutes before time. Gandhi was already there, practicing with one more teammate who was bowling to him at the nets. That showed the level of commitment he had. He was a marvelous batsman and had been trying hard for a couple of years to get selected for Ranji. We went up to him to have a chat. After waiting for a few minutes near the pitch, we got our chance.

"So you two freshers interested in getting into the team, eh? What do you do? Also give me your names," Gandhi rattled off turning towards us after hitting a perfect straight drive.

"Saurabh Singh. I am a batsman, sir," Saurabh said.

"Suhaan Arora. I am a fast bowler and can bat a bit as well," I lied. I knew I was a much better batsman than that but I didn't want to put too much pressure on myself to perform in both the areas. My past experience had also told me that my bowling had an edge over my batting skills.

"Pretty interesting to know that. Why not get over with your selection before everyone else comes in? Here's how it's going to be – Suhaan you'll bowl to Saurabh. If he manages to play it well, then you are out; and if you manage to beat him or get him out, then I'll select you," Gandhi explained.

Saurabh and I looked at each other. We hadn't expected this at all. We had both been dreaming about getting selected in the team together while walking towards the ground. The situation was different now. One had to go back right away. We had no choice but to accept the situation and give it our best. Suddenly, we heard a laugh.

"Hey! I was just messing around with you kids. Just look at your faces!" Gandhi chuckled while giving a high-five to the bowler who had been bowling to him.

Soon, others joined us and the selection began. The ex-students were called to play the role of selectors. They already had seven good players and were looking for two good bowlers, a batsman and a wicketkeeper. First, it was the batsmen's turn to show their skills and Saurabh had lined up for that. The seniors were to bowl to them. One or two batted well, some couldn't handle the pace while others couldn't understand spin bowling. Finally, it was Saurabh's turn. He came in, took his guard and started facing deliveries one after the other. By the time he was done, he had played many of them well, though he got miserably beaten on a few occasions.

The bowlers' turn to show their skills was next. I was given the ball first up, and to my surprise, Gandhi was at the crease waiting to face me. Each bowler could bowl three deliveries and if the selectors liked him, they would ask him to continue. I was confident of bowling well as I had never been out of practice. The only difference was that I used to play with a tennis ball during the break. I counted my run-up and put a small stone as a marker and shouted left arm over-the-wicket. I had a new shining red ball in my hand, the kind I liked the most. I started my run-up and bowled to Gandhi. What happened next was a shock for the selectors, the freshers, and even for Murli kaka, who was one of the cleaners in the campus watching the selection. Gandhi was lying on the pitch in an awkward position. I had bowled him a fast in-swinging delivery on the pads which he had been unable to face. It had crashed onto the stumps. I couldn't hide the grin on my face. Gandhi got up and gave me a thumbs-up, and gestured to me to bowl again. I ran in again, pitched the ball on the exact same spot, but only this time it was an out-swinger. Gandhi couldn't play this one as well; he had edged it and the ball hit the nets behind the stumps. This time Gandhi had a smile on his face. He signaled that I didn't have to bowl anymore. I left happily as I knew there was nothing which could stop me from being in the team. After half an hour, they completed screening the players and announced the names of the four players who had been selected. My name was the first on the list and fortunately, Saurabh had made the cut as well.

"Well done guys! The intra-university tournament begins in a month. Three months later we have the inter-university tournament which will feature all the universities in Gujarat. We'll be practicing daily starting tomorrow morning at seven. Till then, take care and have fun," Gandhi said as everybody started to leave. He stopped me and Saurabh and we had a long chat before going back to our rooms.

That evening, all four of us were at a Café Coffee Day outlet inside the campus, celebrating our selection in the team.

"Great job guys! Way to go," said Akshay, devouring his chicken burger.

"You should have seen the look on Gandhi's face when he fell down after the first delivery you bowled to him. It was as if he had seen pigs flying," quirked Saurabh.

"Naah, I just got lucky because he wouldn't have expected a fresher to bowl with a good pace. It swung in a bit as well."

Meanwhile, Ramaraju was busy ogling at our female classmates and seniors in the cafeteria.

"Take a break, man. Give some rest to your penis. It won't grow by staring at breasts and butts," I said.

"Yeah yeah! As if you can do anything apart from staring at them. How many girlfriends have you had in your entire life, Mr Handsome Hunk? How many chicks have you banged? Or should I ask how many have you even kissed? None, right? Each one of us likes to take a swim in this sea of beauty around us with our eyes. It's just that you rascals hide it and I do it openly," Ramaraju snapped.

"Hahaha, I apologize to thee, O horny one. Please pardon me as I know not what I speak. It's not that I have given it

12

an actual shot, otherwise I could have been sitting on top of a pretty good score by now," I joked.

"And why is that? Are you gay by any chance or just a chicken that does not have the guts to talk to a girl?"

"He was in a boys' hostel all his life; I am putting my money on gay. His ass gets a lot of attention. I have seen girls almost inviting him to sit with them in class and he still doesn't go," Akshay added.

"Hey fat ass! At least I am aware of what I eat," I tried to make fun of him.

"Going in or coming out?" Akshay replied wittily and we burst into laughter.

"I'd like to go with the chicken theory. I have seen him enjoying the admiration he gets from chicks since college started," Saurabh said.

"Okay, enough. What will I have to do to shut you suckers up?" I asked.

"Now that's like a man! Okay listen, can you see that beautiful girl in the corner of the café busy texting on her phone?" Saurabh asked.

"Wow. Who is that?" I couldn't resist asking.

"She is Kanika Banerjee, second year BMS. She is one of the prettiest in the entire university and very popular. Because she is so hot, hardly any guy has had the guts to ask her out till date. All you have to do is go and talk to her for five minutes. Ask her out if you are insane, make her your sister, dance in front of her – your choice! The condition is that you have to spend five minutes with her. By the way, you might want to consider the dancing option as she is also a great dancer and is a part of the college's Arts Circle."

"What? And who's that fatso sitting next to her; she looks like Akshay's sister," I said light-heartedly.

"She is Sanjana, Kanika's roommate," Saurabh said.

"Is Kanika the one in that black spaghetti strap top and denim shorts?" I enquired again as I couldn't digest the fact that I had to face someone as beautiful as her.

"Yep."

"The girl who seems to have just landed from heaven? With her hair undone, natural pink lips and very fair skin?"

"Yeah, dude. Are you going or not?"

"Okay, okay. Did you say she is one of the prettiest and very popular in the college?" I prompted once again in disbelief.

"Okay that's it. Let it be, bro. *Tumse na ho payega.*"

I immediately got up and started walking towards Kanika with my coffee in my hand and half tucking my white shirt into my cherry coloured chinos with my other hand.

"Hey, the place seems a bit full today. Do you mind sharing the table?" I asked Kanika as casually as I could.

Half an hour had already passed since I had joined Kanika and her friend at the table. Saurabh, Akshay and Ramaraju couldn't believe their eyes. I had not seemed that confident even when I was bowling the second ball to Gandhi earlier in the day during the selection! We were smiling, laughing, giving high-fives, talking continuously. We even shared our drinks once. Finally, I stood up and the guys sensed some sanity crawling back into their minds. But that wasn't the case. I sat back right next to Kanika on the same couch! Apparently Kanika wanted to show me something on her phone, and the giggling and laughter continued again. Meanwhile, Saurabh's phone beeped. I had texted him.

"Five minutes your sweet, bootylicious ass."

As if this was not enough, ten minutes later, I got up and left the café with both the girls after paying the bill.

It was becoming impossible for the boys to digest what had just happened. Kanika was the most sought after girl, and I had almost peed my pants as I went up to her. Now we had left the café together. The three of them were looking at each other in shock when I returned.

"Hey, Saurabh. I need the keys of your R15. I am taking Kanika out for a ride," I tapped his back and asked.

Saurabh was still in a state of shock and he just pointed towards the coffee table on top of which the keys were lying.

"Thanks. See you guys later."

I picked up the keys and rushed outside.

They also rushed outside and saw the two of us leaving on Saurabh's sports bike. Finally, they went back to the hostel, still not believing what had happened.

Later that night, Ramaraju was in Akshay and Saurabh's room, waiting for me to return. I reached the hostel late and knocked on the door. Akshay opened it to find me with a grin on my face.

"Thank you guys!" I said as I hugged Akshay. I sprawled on the bed with hands behind my head and closed my eyes.

"Dude, are going to make us beg now?" Ramaraju asked.

"What's there to tell? Everything happened in front of you guys," I said to tease them a bit.

"Oh, come on man. Don't be a jerk now," Saurabh quipped in.

"Alright, alright. You said she was very popular and hardly anyone had asked her out. Being a head-turner, I guessed she wouldn't have too many girlfriends as well. You know, the other chicks think of them as bitches. I had worked all this out. Normal guys like us usually don't get girls like that just because they don't give it a shot and the guys who do ask them in the end are nothing but just pretty faces. From what I sensed, girls like Kanika need someone who could make them laugh and with whom they could feel comfortable. So I just tried to be as natural as I could be. And that's all!" I explained.

"Yeah right! A few hours ago, people were doubting if he was gay and all of a sudden he is a chick magnet explaining his nonsensical philosophies. It was a fluke, bro, admit it!" Akshay said.

"Well, if it was a fluke, it wouldn't have lasted long enough to give me my first kiss," I boasted.

"*What!?*" they all cried in unison.

"Yep. And we even made out a bit on the terrace of the girls' hostel."

"Someone please kill me. I can't take it anymore," Ramaraju said falling on the bed in disbelief.

I then told them about the entire evening with Kanika – everything from the coffee shop to our making out on the terrace and dropping her off.

11.45 p.m.

Kanika walked towards me slowly, with her eyes full of lust. She was wearing a sexy crop top revealing her navel and hot pants. Every passing second seemed like a century to me, I was that desperate for her. She was teasing me by taking her time to get close to me and I was becoming very impatient. Finally, she ran towards me and I took her in my arms. I hugged her as tightly as possible and she held on with all her strength as well. And then we kissed, and kissed madly, with our bodies so close that even air had to take another route to pass. Suddenly, I picked her up, turned, and made her sit on the terrace wall still kissing her. I removed her top and she removed my hooded t-shirt. She was now kissing me all over my chest, neck, biting me at times and caressing me. I then unhooked her bra quickly and wildly snatched it away from her body to expose her tender breasts. My lust now knew no bounds. Her body complimented her beautiful face and pink lips perfectly. I was feeling like the luckiest dog in the world at that moment. I groped her breasts, fondled them, kissed them, sucked her nipples and did whatever I could to calm down the wild beast in me.

"Nobody has ever touched me like this, Suhaan," Kanika moaned.

She then pushed me away and got down from the wall and unzipped my pants, and then hers. And then, we devoured each other's body on the terrace floor. Both entwined in each other, I was thrusting her as softly as I could and we experienced something out of this world.

11.15 p.m.
My phone beeped.

I am craving for your body. Come to me.

It was a text from Kanika.

Now? Why are you doing this to tease me? You very well know boys aren't allowed in the girls' hostel building between ten at night and eight in the morning. Also, the intra-university cricket tournament starts tomorrow so I have to sleep well. We were practicing until two hours ago. Really tired, baby. I replied.

I am not kidding Suhaan. I want to 'go the distance' today. Lusting for you. See you on the terrace in half an hour.

'Go the distance! Did she just text that?' I thought.

Those words were flashing again and again in front of my eyes. I have wanted to go the distance since the moment I saw her the first time and we started dating a month ago, but today it was Kanika who was demanding that. We had made out quite a few times in the past one month, but had never 'gone the distance'.

On the one hand I was jumping with excitement, but at the same time I didn't know how I could meet her. Trying the front door would have been the stupidest option considering the girls' hostel's watchmen, their lady warden, and the bitches who hated Kanika (not just because she was way hotter than them, but also because she was dating me).

What a penis can make a man do is simply amazing. Ramaraju had already slept off. I got out of my room and went to the terrace of my hostel. Both the hostels were separated only by the library building and the gap between the buildings wasn't much. I thought I would check the gap and if possible, would jump to the library building and then to Kanika.

I opened the terrace gate and hurried towards the left wall where the library building was. I bent over a bit and saw the gap. The gap was small but not small enough for me to be able to pull off a Spiderman-like jump. My hope of 'going the distance' was vanishing till I saw a long ladder on the opposite side of the terrace.

"What have you done to me, Kanika? I am putting my life at risk for sex, and I call Ramaraju 'Mr Horny'," I murmured as I picked up the ladder, brought it to the other side and placed it between the boundary walls of both the buildings with their ends resting on the walls.

"*Jai Bajrang Bali!*"

I took the name of the Monkey God and climbed on the wall. I had decided I wouldn't look down and I started taking steps by carefully placing my feet on one rung after the other. Finally, I managed to cross the gap and jumped on the terrace of the library building. I then took the ladder, and repeated the same thing to reach the terrace of the girls' hostel.

12:05 a.m.
"Oh man, your craving really must have been paranormally high today for us to be doing it like this on the terrace," I said.

"Didn't you figure that out during the sex?" Kanika replied naughtily.

"Your wild side was too prominent to miss," I said winking at her.

We were lying on the terrace floor, completely naked after having the time of our lives when we heard a sound.

Screech. Click!

We were lying behind a small partition wall where nobody could see us. Somebody had latched the door and put a lock on it.

"Shit! I think it was the watchman. He must have locked the door," Kanika said in shock.

"What?" I was shocked too.

"Yes, I completely forgot. The watchman locks the terrace door at twelve daily and opens it only at seven in the morning." Kanika said.

"Shit! What do we do now?"

"I have no clue, Suhaan. Do something."

"Can't you ask Sanjana to get it opened?"

"I wish I could. But even if I call Sanjana and ask her to bribe the watchman and get the gate opened, that leech will spread all sorts of nonsense about us and I don't want that. He has seen you dropping me at the front gate many times."

"Okay wait, let me think," I said while putting on my clothes.

I walked towards the library building and started to think about how I could get Kanika out of there.

"Suhaan! Where are my bra and my top? I can't find them," Kanika asked after she wore her pants.

"They must be somewhere around there baby, just look carefully," I said.

It was dark and one could hardly see ten feet ahead clearly.

"Oops! God help me. She is going to kill me for this," I murmured as I looked at the gap between both the buildings. Kanika's clothes were hanging on a cable wire which was going through both the buildings.

I turned and walked backed towards Kanika and told her the whereabouts of her belongings.

"Are you out of your mind? What are you saying? How on earth did that happen?"

"Well I guess when I removed your top and bra you were sitting on the wall and I must have dropped them there by mistake."

"I am going to kill you! What will I do now?" Kanika said while punching me on the chest.

"Don't worry, I've got an idea. Here, take my t-shirt. We'll climb the wall and go to the library building with the help of the ladder. Then you can go down through the library and then back to your hostel. I'll then go to my hostel building and ask Raju to bring a t-shirt for me so that even if my warden sees me getting down from the terrace, he won't be suspicious. Problem solved," I said while removing my t-shirt and giving it to Kanika.

"No way am I climbing that and risking my life."

"Okay then, goodnight. It was nice having sex with you, Ms Banerjee. I'll be leaving now," I started to leave after shaking hands with Kanika like I had completed a business meeting.

"Okay, okay wait, I am coming," Kanika said reluctantly.

We both climbed down the wall and after some hesitancy, Kanika managed to cross to the other side. We jumped and went near the gate. Kanika kissed me and she went off. Then I took the ladder and reached the terrace of my building. I had lost almost all my fear after doing it so many times now. I put my hand in my pocket to take out my phone, but my hands came back empty. I had put my phone in my t-shirt's pocket.

"This can't get any worse," I murmured as I reached the gate and tried to open it. To my surprise, the gate was locked like that of the girls' hostel. I had not anticipated this at all.

"Oh hell! Why are you doing this to me, God? Is this a price I am paying for such awesome sex?" I said sadly, remembering the quote 'all good things come with a price tag'.

Such an ironical night it had been. While I had had the most beautiful experience of my life, I was also paying a handsome price for it. There I was, standing all alone on the terrace with a bare chest on a windy night. There was nothing that I could do apart from sleeping near the terrace gate and waiting for sunrise.

Click! Screech!

I heard a noise which woke me up from whatever little sleep I got the entire night. My eyes were red and were begging for some rest. The practice sessions had been exhaustive since the tournament was nearing and the past day had been one such day. Above that, my midnight heroics had not helped me get any sleep. I waited for a couple of minutes and then ran towards my room praying that the wardens or seniors don't catch me shirtless. Luckily, I reached the room, entered inside and latched it quickly. As soon as I put the latch on the door, I turned and fell on the bed and had almost dozed off when I heard Raju's voice.

"Where the fuck have you been man? Saurabh was asking for you. Even your phone seems to be switched off. Don't you have your match today? You said you made it to the playing eleven, right? It's already seven on the clock. Doesn't' the match start at 7.30?" Raju shot question after question at me.

"Ah! Just stop squeaking, you rat. My head's aching like someone has hit it with a hammer," I snapped back at him. But at the same time I realized what he was saying was right. Gandhi had given me a chance in the playing eleven straight away and it was match time already. I got up and quickly changed into my sports gear and rushed down. I left with a smile, feeling a little surprised because as tough as it may seem to believe, one of the biggest jerks on the planet Ramaraju had showed the sensibility to give a pill for my headache as I was ready to leave.

I managed to reach the ground by at quarter past seven. Gandhi was furious. It had been decided beforehand that I would be leading the bowling attack and Gandhi was in a troubled state of mind when I hadn't turned up. The toss had already taken place and he had opted to bowl first after winning the toss.

"What explanation do you have for this? It better be a very good one!" he asked angrily.

"I couldn't sleep last night so I thought I'll go to the terrace for a while. And while I was lost in thinking about the match, the watchman must have locked the door. I had to spend the entire night up there and could come down into my room only after the watchman opened the gate fifteen minutes ago," I lied.

"Hmmm, we have won the toss and are bowling first. Go, get warmed up quickly."

I heaved a sigh of relief. I was feeling proud of myself for being able to lie so effortlessly, but was still worried about the match. We were playing our first one against a weak dental college team, but I was feeling the pressure because the captain had showed so much confidence in me, and I was in no condition to bowl. It was a knockout tournament; if we lost even a single game, we'd be out.

The NRMC University took its sports very seriously. So there was always a buzz about how a team was doing in a particular game. Cricket, as it goes without saying was the most popular in the university. There were spectators during every match, supporting their teams. To make things worse, our team was a more celebrated and respected team out of the twenty-four teams which were participating because of the team's consistent performance. Our matches definitely drew more crowds. Anyway, I thought it was no point pondering over these thoughts and began to prepare for the match.

The match began. It was a twenty over per side. I didn't bowl well. In fact, I bowled so badly that the captain let me bowl only three of my four allowed overs. They put up a decent score on the board. Luckily for us, they didn't have good bowlers to back it up and we had excellent batsmen. We chased down the total and won the match.

"What were you doing out there today, man? Where was your swing today? Where was the speed? Our next match is with the engineering college day after tomorrow and they are a tougher side to beat. I don't think I can risk it by picking you after what I saw today," Gandhi said angrily after the match.

"Please don't do that. You won't regret picking me for that match. I promise," I pleaded, and after some more pleading, he finally agreed.

I left for the hostel after the bad day on the field. Kanika accompanied me. She was all caring and sorry when she heard about my plight. I dropped her and came back to the hostel and slept off.

I woke up a relieved man in the evening and saw Saurabh and Akshay in the room with Raju. I knew there were going to be a lot of questions, so before any of them could start, I told them what had happened the previous night, skipping the details of the sex, obviously. Akshay congratulated me for the 'feat' I had achieved, whereas Saurabh felt sympathetic. Raju tried hard to get some details out, but I refused to become a medium for him to jerk off.

The next day, I took ample rest and didn't even text Kanika or call. She was miffed about it, but understood later on.

Finally it was time for our match with the engineering students. Gandhi won the toss again and elected to bowl first, only this time I was fit and raring to go. I took my run up and ran in as quickly as I could to the right handed batsman. It was an in-swinger which pitched near the off stump line and hit his pads, very similar to the delivery I had bowled to Gandhi during the selections. I straight away appealed to the umpire for an LBW and he obliged. I had just taken my first wicket in the tournament and I could see how pumped up my teammates were. They had earlier been apprehensive about me getting selected again.

I bowled consistently throughout the innings and ended up picking four wickets. We got them out for a low score and chased it comfortably. I was adjudged 'Man of the Match' and I could finally look Abhishek Gandhi in the eye.

I had found my rhythm and continued to bowl well against one team after the other until we reached the finals. The excitement level was different in that match. My college had won the trophy in the tournament's initial two years and had been reaching the finals since two consecutive years, but hadn't been able to win the tournament. Gandhi was really nervous as he wanted to win more than anyone else.

We played the final against the Physical Education department who were a better side than us. The odds were once again stacked against us as they had played almost supernatural cricket in the past few days. We fortunately managed to beat them comprehensively and won the tournament. Gandhi's joy knew no bounds. He ran across the ground like it was all he had ever wished for in his entire life. I on the other hand was feeling like a star by the end of the tournament too. I was adjudged Man of the Match for the second time in the tournament and more importantly, in the finals. It made me even more popular than whatever little popularity I had gained by dating Kanika.

The tournament had paid rich dividends both on and off the field. I had grabbed all the attention with both hands. Teachers entering the classroom praising me as well as Saurabh to some extent had become a common practice. But with the praises also came a disclaimer that the semester exams were scheduled for the next month and only playing good cricket wouldn't take us through to the second year. We'd have to work really hard from here on to get good grades as we had missed a lot of lectures citing practice, not to mention the bunking.

But the task was only half over yet. The one thing that the entire university really wanted was to win the inter-university trophy which was played between universities from all around Gujarat. It was one thing which had alluded the otherwise crowded trophy rack of the university till now.

As the inter university tournament was beginning right on the first day after our fifteen day semester break, the senior members insisted that Saurabh and I stay back. We were fortunate enough to be shortlisted for the squad as the team for this tournament had the best players from all the departments. My father was rather disappointed to hear that I'd be staying back at first, but he agreed seeing that I was finally taking keen interest in something.

The practice sessions started the next morning and Saurabh and I got engrossed in them completely. We had decided we'd work our asses off to get into the playing eleven of this team because it would be much more difficult as the final eleven would be selected from the entire university and not just our college. We practiced, and practiced really hard. We got all our basics right and worked our plans out. Finally, the names were announced and we were disheartened to know that neither of us had made the cut. The physical education department coach said we were ruled out due to inexperience, as if the experienced guys had done something worth singing praises about. Saurabh was really angry because he was really looking forward to the semester break to visit his hometown Chandigarh. All the hard work had gone in vain, but we thought it had been worth giving it a shot and moved on.

The second semester was a rather quiet one. The only thing which we looked forward to was the college fest. In the past few months, all four of us had developed a strong bond with each other and also with Kanika and Sanjana. We started hanging out more often and enjoyed each other's company. Meanwhile, Kanika and I were cock-a-hoop about our relationship. The terrace of the girls' hostel had witnessed our blissful embrace a couple of times since then.

Soon the entire university had turned from a chaotic cheerful place to a dull and silent one like a crematory with the students moving to and fro slowly with their heads buried in their books. Raju had turned into a maniac. All he would do was study, pray, eat, poop, sleep and repeat the entire cycle. His nature also changed completely as though he was a different person altogether. The guy who would get turned on by anything with a pulse had lost all the interest in girls. I had spotted the hottest of girls passing by him on the way to college and he wouldn't even notice them. Saurabh and Akshay had also been busy. Kanika and I were not being able to spend much time together either. Getting a simple kiss had become like climbing the Everest during this period. Exams were so important in this country that a parent wouldn't mind getting to know that their son is impotent, as much as the neighbour's son scoring three more marks than their son. It can become an issue which can lead to suicidal extents.

The month passed by in the blink of an eye. It brought us within touching distance of the exams in no time. Soon, the exams began and even I got serious and started studying all night. Fortunately, all the papers went well and I was confident that I wouldn't be carrying any load the next year. It was then time for the forty-five day long yearly break. Everybody began packing their bags to leave as early as they could. Ramaraju was hesitant for obvious reasons, and Akshay had already planned to leave for Jaipur, his hometown on the same day that the exams ended.

"Don't go baby. I'll miss you," I joked with Kanika, trying to sound a bit romantic.

"Haha. Don't say that, I am already so low."

She punched my chest slowly with her left hand while the right one was busy fiddling with the phone with no intention to call, message or do anything else for that matter. She had been sad since the time we had sat in the taxi to leave for the airport. She was going back to Delhi by a late night flight and I was accompanying her to the airport like a good boyfriend.

"Hey, it's only a month-and-a-half. It'll pass just like that, Juliet. Romeo will meet you right here when you return."

"Yeah yeah. It's just that I'll miss the sex like anything," she said.

"As if we do it every night or something; only thrice and that too, how!" I chuckled.

"The scarcity of it is what has made me want it even more."

We reached the airport in time for her flight and after getting her luggage out from the boot, she held me close and kissed me. Right in front of the taxi driver, the other taxi drivers, the people...oh so many people! She did it like we were alone there. She looked into my eyes for a second, turned in the next and walked away inside the building in the next few without looking back even once.

"*Chale, Sahib?*" the taxi driver asked me to sit in the car to get back to the university. He was grinning from ear to ear after what he had seen. It was *his* cheeks which had turned red instead of mine. He was looking happier than me. A person who hadn't seen me in the act would have definitely pointed him out as the receiver of the kiss.

What had happened had got me thinking though. It was not expected of someone like Kanika. Ours was a very casual relationship and we hadn't made any commitments to each other. Things would become very awkward if we were at different places in this relationship. I really enjoyed her company and I also enjoyed hanging out with Sanjana. An awkward situation with Kanika would definitely affect my friendship with Sanjana as well. I didn't want any of this to happen. Things were perfect the way they were.

"*Pauch gaye, Sahib,*" the driver said as we reached the university. I was so lost in my thoughts that I hadn't realize when we had left the airport and reached college. I went to my room and slept off. The next morning, I left for home.

I took the key out from my pocket and put it inside the lock and opened the room's door.

"Kanika!" I said aloud in shock. She was sitting in my hostel room, looking pretty in a skirt and a tank top.

"Weren't you supposed to return from Delhi tomorrow? And how did you manage to get into the room?" I enquired. Before I could shoot anymore questions, she hurried towards me and we kissed, and we kept doing it till I somehow managed to latch the door.

"To answer your questions now, I was getting bored at home so I decided to return early and surprise you. And I knew Raju was reporting this afternoon so I took the keys from him and asked to make himself scarce for the rest of the evening," she explained while we were lying naked on my bed.

"Well I must say you've done a great job," I winked.

"So how were your holidays? Missed me?" she asked.

"It always feels good to go home. I am at peace and feel like I can do whatever I want. Sometimes I'd go to the club for a nice swim, sometimes I'd play a bit of squash and at times I'd just stay home and take long naps. There's nothing like it when Mom is around taking care of me."

"Yeah, whatever," she said and turned to the other side and started fiddling with her phone.

"Haha, of course I missed you," I said and hugged her tightly for the moment, but my mind was totally somewhere else. The questions which my mind was asking me after we had that kiss at the airport still had not been answered. Yes, we hadn't been in much contact during the summer break apart from one or two Skype chats and a couple of 'sexting' sessions, but it didn't clear anything per se. So I finally gathered courage and decided to ask her.

"Hey baby," I started of what could be a very uncomfortable conversation.

"Hmm?"

"Is everything okay between us?"

"Yeah, why?"

"No, just asking." I gave a wry smile and gave her a peck on the lips.

"What's wrong, Suhaan?" she asked, now looking into my eyes.

"Okay, here it is. The way you were behaving when I dropped you at the airport before the holidays was nothing like you, and then that courageous kiss. I just wanted to make sure we are on the same page in this relationship," I took my time, hesitated and let the words out of my mouth carefully.

"Just look at your face! Are you insane? I am most certainly not dreaming about the future Mrs Kanika Arora and she giving birth to your kids or something. I told you I'll miss the sex and the dullness was due to that only. I obviously love spending time with you and we chicks are a bit on the sentimental side. I was in that mood the other night. So chill!" Kanika winked.

"God! That's such a relief. So now that everything is sorted out, you ready for round two?"

"Don't you like her?" Kanika asked.

"Yeah, I do, but I know she won't go out with me," Akshay said, still staring at her.

"You are just assuming that. Come on, fatty, don't tell me you are going to give up without even trying," Kanika said trying to encourage him.

"Well it certainly seems like it."

"I think you should borrow some confidence from Suhaan. Did he look like he had a chance with someone like me? And look, here I am sitting next to you after one year with this guy already," she took a dig and started laughing looking at me.

It was amazing how she could be so casual with Akshay when the guy was dripping his shirt wet with sweat and his pants with you know what.

"Oh yeah, when he can do it, why can't I? That's a big positive in the confidence department, Kanika. Thanks."

"See, now we are talking. Now go and get your girl!" Kanika said cheering Fatty up.

We were all sitting in the coffee outlet of the library building during the lunch break. Akshay was crazy about this transfer student who had joined only this year. It had been two months and all Akshay was doing was constantly staring at her whenever he got a chance. He had attended more classes in the past two months than in the entire previous year combined. But the most important thing to notice was that he'd even forget his meals at times if there was a scope for more staring. I, Saurabh and even Ramaraju had managed to talk to her a few times, but not Fatty. Last night, we had finally convinced him to grow a pair of balls and go talk to her. Yes we could understand Fatty's concerns as she was an above average girl in the looks department. She was slim, and had a wheatish complexion.

"Let me tell you something, lady. One week I roam around single and I'll have at least a dozen proposals. So don't give me the lucky dog tag," I snapped back at Kanika after Akshay left on his quest.

"Oh you stud you! Baby is crying; does he need a lollipop?" she said pouting her lips and gave me a kiss on the cheek like one would do to a small kid. Saurabh, Ramaraju and Sanjana giggled.

"Guys hurry up, we need to pack," Akshay said when he returned after a few minutes.

"Excuse me! Check please," he told the waiter.

"What?"

"Pack for what?"

"Pack what?"

"Why hurry up?"

We all responded in different ways.

"I'll tell you on the way to the hostel building. Now get up."

"Yeah, but will you at least tell us what happened with Mehr? And why is she leaving all of a sudden?" Kanika asked him.

"Okay, here it is. I started off the conversation alright, but after two minutes into it, I didn't have anything to say. So I asked her if she would like to join me and my friends for a trip to Goa this weekend."

"*What?*"

This time, we all responded in unison.

"Yeah, and to my shock, she said yes. And now, we are all leaving for Goa by the evening flight today and she is bringing a friend with her as well. So hurry!"

"Are you out of your freaking mind? We can't just go like this. And what do you mean she said yes? Have I teleported to USA somehow? Do such things happen so causally in India? Where is the country going?" Saurabh blurted out in shock.

"Haha, take it easy Saurabh Uncle. I agree it's not something which we see every day, but now that it has happened, I think we should definitely go," Sanjana said.

"Yeah please let's go Suhaan. It'll be fun," Kanika insisted.

"I wish we could, but the tournament is coming up and we have practice sessions."

"Let's go to Goa and we can have massage sessions," Kanika winked. The prospect of an exotic massage was enough for Saurabh and Raju to agree as they nodded their heads in approval.

"It's just two nights. How much difference can it make? Please, let's go no baby," she requested trying to imitate the cute little pussy from the *Shrek* movie series, whom no one in the world could say no to.

What next? We were at the airport waiting for our boarding to be announced.

"Careful, baby. Now come out slowly, one leg at a time," said Kanika while helping me out of the car outside the hostel building.

"*Arey ye kya hogaya beta?*" asked a concerned Murli Kaka as he saw me limping and rushed towards our cab. I had met with an accident in Goa while riding a bike. It happened just after Kanika and I had won shit loads of money in the casino while returning to the hotel. Luckily, Kanika was sitting pillion with Sanjana on her moped and hence didn't get injured along with me. My body was covered with bruises all over. Moreover, I had fractured my right arm. The doctor had said the bruises would stop hurting in a few days, but the plaster would stay on for three weeks at least.

Saurabh, Akshay and Ramaraju promised the girls that they'd take care of me and sent them off to the girls' hostel. After much effort, the boys managed to take me to my room and made me lie down on the bed. I was furious with myself and was feeling really low because an injury for three weeks meant I would miss both the intra as well as the inter university tournament. The latter did have some time in between, but the doctor had asked me to stay away from rigorous physical activity for at least ten weeks. By then, the squads would be finalized.

I was on complete bed rest for the next few days. The guys took great care of me and I recovered well. I went back to college from the next week onwards. Meanwhile, the selections were done with and the tournament began. Shridhar Chauhan, the new captain after Gandhi, almost had a heart attack after hearing about my injury. I was supposed to be the team's main bowler and now I wouldn't be able to play even a single game the entire season. To make things worse, another fast bowler in the team was down with jaundice. Shridhar was crestfallen after that. The absence of quality players reflected in the performance and we didn't even reach the semi finals that year.

One man's loss is another man's gain. The famous saying had a twist in its execution for me though. Not being able to play cricket was a huge loss for me, but at the same time, staying in the room with Ramaraju for long durations gave me time to study much more than usual and I wrote almost all the papers perfectly. I was pretty confident about getting good grades.

The plaster was removed when it was time for the winter break. I had started with a bit of exercise to bring my right arm back to duty.

All the students were busy doing something or the other during the start of the next semester. The studious ones had started preparing for CAT and other such competitive exams. The ones interested in sports had started concentrating on their competitions lined up ahead. The campus recruitments were creating a buzz whereas I had nothing to do but stroll from one part of the college to the other. I wasn't going to any of these because I just could not see myself doing a nine to six job at this point of my life. I was ready to join my father if nothing else worked out, but this was a strict no. Even Kanika was busy with the college fest.

"What? You must be crazy to even think that! No way am I doing it!" I rejected sternly. We were sitting in the library cafeteria.

"Oh come on, don't be such a pussy. At least give it a try! I promise, if you don't find it convincing, I won't force you and you'll be free to go," Kanika pleaded.

One of the two lead actors of the play, which was to be performed by the Arts Circle in the college fest, had backed out due to a tiff with the director citing issues about the length of his role. The team was searching for a replacement and Kanika was bold enough to suggest my name. Moreover, she had effortlessly lied that I was a regular participant in my school's drama team when the truth was I wasn't even remotely associated with it.

"You seriously think it's a joke, don't you? Acting is just not my cup of tea. You do not know the level of my stage fright. My teacher had forced me to do it once when I was a kid and let me tell you, till today I have nightmares about that day. Hundreds of people staring at me, waiting to laugh at my minutest mistake and judge every move of mine makes me feel very uncomfortable. It feels like I am a lone soldier in a war standing in front of an entire army waiting to blow my body into little pieces of flesh," I explained.

"Blah Blah Blah! Stop being such a chicken. Now come on, let's give it a shot. The drama team is doing a play inspired by Shakespeare's tragic play 'Julius Caesar'. The original play is quite lengthy and needs a lot of time. They have given it an Indian twist to shorten it and made it a bit funny as well. The script is looking quite impressive now. If selected, you'll be playing the role of Antony," she said before pausing to take a sip of her coffee.

"Keep going," I said.

"You'll have to prepare his dialogues for the audition so that the directors get a picture of how you would fit in."

"You are just making your case worse with each sentence, my lady. I've read the play during my school days and Antony's is the central and the most difficult character to portray. I am pretty sure I am not doing it. Thank you for the offer," I said getting up and started to leave. I had to rush to the bank to complete a couple of transactions for Dad.

"Alright, don't do it. Almost two years of being with you and I don't have the right to ask for a small audition. It just proves how much you love me and care for my feelings. But it's okay,

I understand how difficult it must be for you. I'll just go and apologize to the director even though he was counting on me," she began blackmailing me emotionally with her eyes getting moist.

"Aww, please don't cry, baby. I'll do it."

I knew I was doomed, but one has to pay a price for having such a hot girlfriend.

The audition was supposed to take place the very next morning. I had started reliving Antony's pain on Caesar's death and had started memorizing the lines after getting back to my room. Remembering the lines weren't as important as expressing them in the right manner. Kanika had Antony's famous speech ready with her and was there to help me till the time she was allowed to stay, but eventually she had to leave. Raju had started staying in the library till late to prepare for the entrances, so I was all by myself in the room.

"Friends, Romans, and Countrymen…"

I began to act after memorizing half the speech. It sounded stupid to me as the words came out. I couldn't imagine how the director would take it. The speech itself was such a lengthy one and was also considered as one of Shakespeare's greatest works ever. But I didn't give up. I watched a few videos of the play which had been enacted before on YouTube and it helped me a great deal. I started again and went on doing it until I dozed off and woke up the next morning with Kanika's call.

We were late by twenty minutes for the audition. Kanika had been a part of the Art Circle since two years so we were allowed inside without any fuss.

"That's Baldy, my classmate and the director of the play," Kanika said pointing towards an almost bald and fat guy sitting in the front row and watching the audition with two other guys.

"That joker is the director! By the way, I see where he gets his name from." I giggled.

"Shut up. That's because his name is Baldev Singh. The baldness is just a coincidence."

I saw a fresher reciting the lines which I had practiced. He had a squeaky voice. The team of judges didn't hesitate one bit in making it pretty clear to the guy that he couldn't act. They laughed right on his face; Baldy almost fell off his chair. I was next and was quite confident about landing in the same spot as the monkey-voiced. I was getting really nervous and Kanika could see it.

"Listen to me very carefully, Suhaan. Forget that there are three judges sitting in front of you. Get the feeling of that lone soldier out of you and just feel Antony's situation. You have captained a cricket team and you must have given many a motivational speeches to your team before important matches. Antony's situation is the same here. He just has to motivate the crowd to punish Caesar's killers. Now go, and rock it!" Kanika motivated me.

It certainly made me feel good as I started taking the steps towards the centre stage. I reached the centre, closed my eyes, imagined that there were hundreds of people in front of me and began my speech after opening my eyelids.

"Friends, Romans, countrymen, lend me your ears; I come to bury Caesar, not to praise him. The evil that men do lives after them; the good is oft interred with their bones; so let it be with Caesar as well. Brutus had told you that Caesar was ambitious and if that was the case, it was a horrendous crime, and he faced an apt punishment for it, and he received from Brutus, who is an honourable man. Caesar was faithful…" I started the speech. I had managed to memorize the entire thing but hadn't managed to practice enacting it.

"*My friends, I do not wish to stir you up to such a sudden flood of mutiny. The honourable men who have killed Caesar, I do not know what grief they had which made them...*"

"Enough!" Baldev said and asked me to stop when I had reached only halfway.

"I had asked the participants to memorize the lines of Antony's speech, not to blabber whatever pleases them," he said in a serious tone. I was so lost in the mood that I had started making up my own lines! Yes, I was enacting the scene properly and my lines had the same meaning in general, but they were not even remotely close to Antony's.

The chance of getting selected for the role was gone. Not that I was dying to do it, but the stamp of getting rejected would be painful.

"But even after that, you've managed to get into the character so well, and that has impressed me beyond bounds. It was as if I was standing on the streets of Rome and could feel the pain," he said and started clapping. The other two judges followed, and then the other participants. I couldn't believe what was happening. They were praising me for something which I thought I sucked at.

"It'll be a pleasure to work with you. Welcome aboard!" Baldev said while climbing on the stage and shaking hands with me. Kanika strode towards me and hugged me.

The inter university tournament again ended on a sour note. The team did well to reach the finals as the players from the Physical Education department performed well, but lost the match after a close fight. Once again, the team was left wanting for the title.

The rehearsals for the play, on the other hand, had been going on continuously. It was a very different experience from that of cricket. Cricket was more like short bursts of aggressiveness wherein one would put all their strength to enhance their skills. And the drama practices were more like a hangout with your seniors as well as juniors; they would start after the college at around seven in the evening and go on till late in the night, sometimes even past midnight. Food would then be ordered from outside and the scenes discussed while eating. A lot of leg pulling and pranks during the rehearsals were a common practice. Kanika was with the dance troupe and not a part of the play per se, but both our units would often hang out and have small parties. I was having a really good time with my new-found friends. Moreover the play with Baldev's modifications was shaping up into a great one.

The three day college fest had begun in full swing. Finally, the evening which we all had been waiting for arrived. The play was set-up in the humungous open auditorium. It had a big, circular stage at the centre rising about two feet above the ground and there were these huge stairs surrounding three-fourths of the circular stage for the audiences to sit and revel in the plays. It wasn't much of a competition, but more like a one-off play; so the pressure to compete with others wasn't there. But what was bothering me the most was the tussle which was going on in my mind. It was a fight between disaster and glory. Questions like – Would I be able to remember all the dialogues? Would I be able to deliver them aptly? Would I be able to complement other veterans who have been doing it since their school days? – were haunting me. Another part of my heart was also contemplating how would I react if the dean called my name for a special praise? How would I react to all the accolades from the hot chicks and the envious looks from the guys like it had happened during the cricket tournament days. The nightmares about not performing well had a clean advantage over their counterparts though.

The play began, and went off very well. I almost got blank in one or two instances, but my co-actors helped by hinting and giving me leads for the next dialogues. The forty-five minute long play ended in time, and the audience looked happy. The entire team was lauded for its efforts, especially Baldy for managing to pull it off while tampering with such a historic piece of art. All in all, it was a great experience but I had promised myself never to do it again as this sort of pressure was a bit too much for me to handle.

"I think it's going to be quite difficult for him," Saurabh said.

"Yeah dude, even I think so. They've been together like shoes and laces for two years. I wonder how they'll manage it now," Akshay said.

"Shoes and laces? Who uses that kind of a metaphor? And whom are we discussing here?" Mehr asked as she and Sanjana walked up to the coffee table where Saurabh, Ramaraju and Akshay were seated at the college library. It was exam time in NRMC and the students were done with all the subjects, except theone which was due the next day. Kanika and Sanjana were their seniors and it was to be their last day in college.

"Suhaan and Kanika, who else?" Akshay answered.

"I almost cried last night when Sanjana and I were discussing them," Mehr said with her eyes getting moist again.

"Silly girls and their silly tears! They'll manage baby, just relax!" Akshay said wrapping a huge piece of flesh which he called his hand around her shoulder.

"They'll have to stay away from each other at least for a year. Kanika is going to the US for her further studies. Will Suhaan also attend college there in the future just to be with her?" Sanjana probed.

"He could go there for the sex for sure. Kanika is so hot after all," Ramaraju quipped.

"Oh, shut up you pervert," Mehr said disgusted.

"Let's try and talk to him and get to know what's on his mind before the party which he has planned after the exam tomorrow," Saurabh said.

"Sounds good. Meanwhile, Sanjana and I will try and pacify Kanika."

I had booked a few rooms in the Hyatt Regency, Ahmedabad for everyone for the next day. The plan was to get together in one room and smoke, drink, roll a few joints and dance all night to celebrate our friendship and to bid goodbye to Kanika and Sanjana. As drinking was illegal in Gujarat, it took me some courage to arrange the stuff from Daman, a union territory near Gujarat, also popularly known as 'mini Goa' because of its beaches and easy booze availability.

We were done with the exam by evening the next day. Saurabh and I went to meet the seniors in the team and then met our classmates with Raju and Akshay. I left the university early to make some arrangements for the party and asked the guys to join me directly at the hotel. Everything worked out as planned and the booze and other stuff reached our rooms hassle free. We partied hard. Akshay had done a tremendous job with the music. We had to keep the volume a bit low but we danced on every number from *Dhinka Chika* to *Summer of 69* and from Akcent's *That's my name* to Sunny paaji's *Mai nikla, O gaddi leke*. We got to witness a Ramaraju special on *Lungi Dance*. After the girls were high, we were lucky enough to witness a sensuous performance on a remix of *Kajra re* and a hit number from the band Pussycat Dolls. We partied till three in the morning. Saurabh and Akshay were sharing a room and so were Sanjana and Mehr. Ramaraju had requested for a separate room for reasons best known to him. Kanika was happy high and so was I. We had the best sex in two years that night. It was something else.

All the guys were standing at the reception desk with gloomy faces the next morning.

"Hey, how are you feeling man? I know it must be quite difficult for you," Saurabh said placing his hand on my shoulder.

"Feeling about what? What must be difficult for me?" I asked surprised. I had just returned from the hotel gate after seeing Kanika and Sanjana off. Kanika had insisted on not taking the trouble to come all the way to the airport.

"Oh, don't pretend to be strong. I know you must be dying from inside," Saurabh continued.

"I don't have a clue what you are talking about. Would you please care to elaborate?"

"Kanika, man! We are all worried about you two. How are you guys going to manage things with her gone now? Plus you guys haven't been talking about it with anybody else."

"We are not going to manage anything, bro," I said.

"What do you mean?"

"We are not going to try and manage anything. We just broke up with each other," I said very casually.

"What? Why?" they all said in unison.

"Relax guys! What's with the sad, shocked, and tensed expressions? We both knew we wouldn't be able to handle the long distance nonsense and had decided that we'd part our ways at least a couple of weeks ago. We aren't the Laila-Majnu couple that you've been imagining. Chill guys! It was just a casual affair!" I explained.

"Fuck you! And we've been sick worrying about you two!" Mehr said.

"Who has a casual affair for two years? And how can you be so much at ease after breaking up? Was it only about sex for you two?" Akshay said, supporting his girlfriend.

"God! Why are you guys acting like eighty-year-olds? Yes, there was a sense of attachment between us and I will definitely miss her. Though I can't deny the fact that sex was also an integral part of our relationship, but the bigger picture is that being in a committed long distance relationship would have brought with it more bad than good. So we decided we'd try and stay friends, with no strings attached."

"Welcome to the new, practical world folks! Here, even the dictionary doesn't know what 'feelings' mean. It would just show a syntax error if you searched for it," Akshay said irritated.

They were all a bit surprised after hearing what I had to say, but after a bit of explaining they did seem to agree with me except for Akshay. Mehr got sentimental after hearing how casual we were about it and she made Akshay promise to be together with her forever. I escaped being hit on the eye by his jumbo sized left shoe when we returned to our rooms to complete the formalities to check-out.

"Great bowling, Suhaan, keep it up," the wicketkeeper of our team said.

We were practicing for the inter university tournament during the winter break of our final year. The past six months had been quite eventful. After gaining full recovery of my arm, I had started hitting the gym on a regular basis and it had become my new-found passion. Also, I had started playing regular cricket since the summer break and it had shown its results in the intra university competition. I was bowling at a much higher speed and at the same time with a lot of accuracy as well. I had started feeling a lot fitter and to my delight, even a couple of abs had started taking their shape.

Things had changed a lot since I first came to the college. I still remember the day when Saurabh and I had given our best to get selected in the team and today, we were the selectors. Saurabh was appointed the captain of the team due to his consistent performances for the past two years. The championship was supposed to begin the next day and I had a feeling that this was finally going to be the year when we'd bring the trophy home.

The tournament began in full swing. We started taking down one team after another. Our performance was exceptional. No opposition team had even crossed the 100 run mark in a 20-20 game. We had taken all the opposition's wickets in each of our games and I was leading the bowling attack well. A total of sixteen teams were participating in the tournament and it was a knockout tournament, which meant we had to be on our toes all the time. One bad day could kick us out. The positive side was that we just needed to win four matches to lift the trophy. We had almost bullied the first three teams we faced and had reached the finals quite comfortably.

"Some Shubendhu Bose is going to be the chief guest this year and they are saying the event has become more popular due to it. Who is he?" I asked Saurabh on the morning of the finals.

We were up against Ahmedabad University, the defending champions. The match was to take place in one of their college grounds.

"You don't know who Shubendhu is! Man, if you are a cricket fan you have to know who he is," Saurabh said.

"Will you cut the drama and just tell me please?"

"He is the coach of the Gujarat Ranji cricket team."

"And that seems like a big deal to you? There are so many teams who play Ranji and one can't be blamed for not knowing their coaches."

"Let me at least finish my sentence, you asshole. Being the coach is just his job on paper. He means much more than that. He has a say in the national selection of players too. He is a sort of a bridge between the players' dreams and reality to play international cricket. He keeps an eye on every Ranji player, and during the selection committee meetings, his word is often weighed heavily due to his vast experience. He himself could have been an instant entry into the Indian cricket team but he had suffered a knee injury which kept him out of the scene forever," Saurabh explained.

The toss went against us and we were asked to bat first. We couldn't capitalize on a good start given by the openers and were bundled out for a paltry score of 97. Thank god for the 53 runs partnership between me and Saurabh, or else our scorecard would have looked much uglier. The onus was now on me and the other bowlers to take us over the line.

"Left-arm over the wicket," I told the umpire as I started to take my run-up.

"It's going to be an in-swinger around his pads, give me a short mid-wicket and deep square leg," I directed Saurabh and he obliged. I was ready to open the bowling after fifteen minutes of the innings break. The coach had given us a Shahrukh-like speech from the movie *Chak de India* which had boosted our confidence. I ran in and bowled with all the pace that I could. It resulted in the batsman just about managing to get the bat in between the ball and the pads.

"Out-swinger next. Let the field be the same," I told Saurabh. *"Howzzaaat?"*

We all appealed and the umpire raised his finger in a flash. The ploy had worked. The batsman was expecting another in-swinger but to his surprise, it went away from him and he edged it to the keeper. We had our first wicket and that was just the start we wanted.

Next up, I rolled my arm with all the strength I had and delivered a fast, toe-crushing yorker to the next batsman and it crashed onto the stumps. We had their second wicket and we knew we had sent a message to the opposition that this game was far from over. The next batsman was Naved, their left-handed star batsman. With 171 runs from just three matches, he was the highest scorer in the tournament. I knew if we could get him out cheaply, we'd put them under serious pressure. I had three slips and a short cover placed for him. I wanted him to feel the pressure. I ran in, bowled a length delivery on the middle stumps, and made it swing a bit late towards his off-stump.

"*Bowled him!*" I roared and stood in the middle of the pitch with my arms aloft. The tip of his off-stump was murdered by the ball and the stump had gone cart-wheeling. I was mauled by my teammates as they knew how important this wicket was. Moreover, to my delight, I had picked up a hat-trick!

At the end of the first over, the scorecard read 0/3. We could not have asked for anything better than this. The other bowlers gained a lot of confidence and we started to bowl well with each other in tandem. The Ahmedabad University never came back into the game after that and we won the match and the tournament comprehensively. I managed to pick two more wickets and my bowling figures at the end of the match were 3.4-2-4-5, which meant I had bowled 3.4 overs with two maidens, given away 4 runs in all and picked up 5 wickets. As soon as I took the last wicket, the scenes at the ground were something to see. We had a lot of support this time and the crowd was celebrating. All my teammates were jumping over each other in joy. The stumps were uprooted to be taken home as souvenirs. We had been coming so close to winning it over the years but had never managed to; and here we were, the champions standing in the middle of the ground and soaking in all the admiration.

It was time for the ceremony and I was adjudged Man of the Match for scoring some crucial runs and picking up 5 wickets. The award was presented by none other than Mr Shubendhu Bose himself.

"Well done, Suhaan. Keep up the good work. Meet me after the presentation ceremony is over. I would like to have a little talk with you," he said as he handed over the small trophy.

Mr Bose then handed over the championship trophy to Saurabh. There were loud roars once again.

"You wanted to talk to me, Sir?" I went running to Mr Bose as soon as we were done with the celebration. Interestingly, he was waiting for me near the boundary rope with a couple of other people.

"You guys carry on, I'll join you in a bit," he told the guys standing with him.

"I must say that was one amazing spell of fast bowling. What club do you play for?" he asked putting his hand around my shoulders as we started to take a walk around the ground.

"No club, Sir. I just play it for fun," I said.

"Oh is it? Then what is your future plan, young man? Do you belong to the nerd vine? And it's Bose da, not Sir. It makes me sound like I'm some class teacher."

"No... Not really, Bose da, though I have been preparing a bit for the MBA entrance exams with my nerd friend Raju. But it's just a go with the flow thing," I said after I paused for a couple of seconds to control my laughter. The reason was his informal name Bose da which sounded like a Hindi slang.

"Well, then why don't you start taking cricket seriously? Start playing for a club and see how it goes from there?" he suggested.

"Err...professional cricket? I don't think I can match that level. I just play because I love the sport; I've never looked at it from that angle," I explained.

"Well, my boy, the spell you bowled over there was one of the very best I've seen in recent years. Moreover, you are quite a batsman too. I don't think I can give you a better push than that. Think about it. Give a trial for GCA Club House and let me know. I'll take it from there."

"Sure Sir, err, I mean Bose da," I said hesitantly.

"Hey, what's up man? Quite a chat you were having there with Bose da," Saurabh asked as I came back.

"Well, he thinks I can go a long way and was asking me to start playing professional cricket!"

"Great! You lucky dog! What wrong have I done in life to see all this? He is a last bencher in school but somehow gets into NRMC; he dates the hottest chick in the college, and now this. You gotta be kidding me God!" Saurabh exclaimed.

"Well, he actually did. He was all praises about my performance and asked me to give a trial for the GCA Club House, though I am not too sure about it."

"Are you nuts? There are at least ten thousand cricket aspirants who'll do anything to get a chance to play at a good level, whereas when one of the head honchos of the association is giving you that opportunity embellished on a plate, you are acting all naive. Trust me, Suhaan, don't let this opportunity go," Saurabh said.

Saurabh did have a point. Cricket was a religion in this country and there was a sea of youngsters trying for a state level player status if not a national berth. And there was a word around that just talent doesn't do it for you; you have to be prepared for some investment.

"Okay, I'll do it," I finally agreed and we hugged.

The next couple of months were routine for me. I went for the trials and fortunately my performance was good enough, at least according to me. Bose da did the rest by putting in a word for me. He had told me the very first day that he wouldn't use his influence for me and I'll have to prove my worth. He would just ask the selectors to look at me more attentively. I had gotten into a habit of being with Kanika after two years with her and I did miss her. More so because of the dry run I was having. I did go on a few dates with a couple of other girls after that, but nothing materialized.

Soon, the exams came and passed by in a flash. Three years had gone by like three days. The mood was pretty somber. Nobody wanted to leave college as we had had a great run together and none of us was ready to accept the fact that there wouldn't be any more of it. But we have to accept whatever destiny plans for us. We decided to move on with our lives with a promise to meet at least once a year, no matter what.

After college, I joined the GCA Club House and started playing regularly for them. It was cricket and only cricket for me. I would occasionally meet a few school and college friends, but it was cricket which kept my spirits up. I did appear for a few MBA entrance exams as a backup, but I wasn't too hopeful about any of them. Eight months had passed since I had passed out from college when one day, I received a call.

"Suhaan! How are you man? Long time!"

It was Akshay.

"Hey Fatty! How have you been? I am good, I am good; you tell me," I replied. Akshay had joined his father's business after college. After some catching up, he broke the news.

"Okay listen, here's the news. You remember Mehr?" Akshay asked.

"Yep, fatso's hot girlfriend with an awesome ass. You were one lucky bastard I must say. Anyway, what about her?"

"Watch it, bro, I am getting married to her next month," he said.

"Okay, what is it with you giving me breaking news every time you open your mouth! I mean, are you serious? How can you be serious? For God's sake, we are not even twenty-three yet! Who gets married at this age?" I posted a flurry of questions in shock.

"Relax, bro, I didn't have an option…"

"Yes that is something I can agree upon, but still you could have waited for at least another year or so…"

"Bro, you are not listening to me. Hear me out. Mehr is pregnant."

"*What*! Pregnant? What do you mean by pregnant? How can you get her pregnant? I mean, are you serious? How can you be serious? For God's sake! Who gets pregnant at this age? What were you thinking?"

I almost skipped a heartbeat.

"It was just a spur of the moment thing man. We were still going strong with each other. She was in Kolkata for some work some time back and I had just gone to visit her at her hotel. Things spiced up a bit and I didn't have a condom with me. She had a plane to catch after an hour and so we decided to do it anyway. A few days later, she took the test and the unexpected happened. She was so petrified with the positive result that she forgot to dump the strip. Unfortunately, the test strip got into the hands of her mother and then, the families got involved. And here we are, me inviting you to my freaking wedding!" Akshay explained.

"You are so screwed, so fucking screwed!"

I landed at the Rajiv Gandhi International Airport in
Shamshabad, Hyderabad and was waiting at belt number
three to collect my luggage. The wedding was supposed to
take place at the Ramoji Film City. Spread over 2000 acres,
it is the largest integrated film city in the world. Akshay and
Mehr's families must have definitely spent a fortune to organize
the wedding there. One could get an idea from the invitation
card which the guests had received. It was grandeur personified.
As I moved out of the airport, the person holding the placard
with my name on it escorted me to the car. After almost an
hour's drive, I reached the gates of Ramoji Film City. They were
huge and akin to an entrance to a castle. A few minutes later, I
reached the lobby of Sitara Hotel. I and a few other guests who
had reached simultaneously were welcomed with drums and
garlands. Akshay was waiting there to welcome everybody and
to my surprise, Saurabh was standing next to him. We danced
for a while to the drumbeats before checking into our rooms.
The event management team had gone to another level and had
done everything to make the wedding lavish and at the same
time make every guest feel special. It seemed there were more
event management people in the hotel than the hotel staff. The
corridors on each floor had a banner standing with a support

which read one of the seven vows of the Hindu wedding ritual. Quite ironically, the hotel had exactly seven floors.

"Our room is on the left. Yeah, that's the one," Saurabh said as we walked along the corridor of the third floor to locate our room.

There was a beautiful basket wrapped with a light pink ribbon kept on the bed which contained a few snacks, a couple of cold drinks and a pill for headaches. They were quite obviously anticipating there was going to be a lot of drinking and hangovers. There was a scroll as well with the itinerary written on it.

21st February

1:00 p.m.
Carnival and Tomatino festival followed by lunch at Princeton Street.
4:30 p.m.
High-Tea @ Sitara Restaurant
7:00 p.m.
Tilak followed by Sangeet.
10:00 p.m.
Bollywood Night with DJ

22nd February

9:30 a.m.
Pool Party
1:00 p.m.
Punjabi themed lunch with Bhangra-Shangra at Gulmohar Garden
4:00 p.m
High-Tea

6:00 p.m.
Baraat
8:00 p.m.
Reception @ Mughal Garden
9:30 p.m.
Sufi Night

23rd February
Breakfast and departure

We had reached the hotel room 12.30, so we quickly got dressed for the carnival and left for Princeton Street. It was a three-minute drive from the hotel. It was a street made of artificial bungalows which were used in movies. They were made of wood rather than concrete. I remembered it from when I visited it for the first time during a school trip to the film city.

As soon as we reached, I was taken by surprise by what I was seeing. An otherwise normal street with row houses on both sides of the road had been given a complete festive look. There were these long pieces of colorful clothes hanging from the top of the bungalows to the others across the street. There was a stall with props like funny hats, masks, overly sized goggles, and bandanas. Then there were a couple of Moko Jumbies, a few hot Russian dancers in glittery dresses and wings dancing to the loud but pleasant music, a couple of counters with funny dummies of cars and famous monuments where you could get your photos clicked. As we moved further into the street, we could see at least a dozen food counters serving cuisines from all around the world, a dance floor, and an open bar. Finally a huge area in the shape of a square surrounded by a wooden boundary around two feet high on all sides with a small entrance on one was revealed to us. It was filled at least with a million tomatoes and was ready to soak in as many humans as possible and paint them red.

"Hey friends!" a voice called out. The moment we heard it, we knew it was Ramaraju.

"Hey! What took you so long man? Akshay said you'll be here before us."

He had become thinner in the past few months.

"The flight got delayed."

"So, still a pervert? Or have you found someone?" I asked.

"Well, I just can't seem to betray the first love of my life – my right hand," he said, much to our disgust.

We then moved around the place and started to have fun. Sanjana had joined us as well. Only Kanika couldn't make it to the wedding. We were at the bar beginning to have our drinks when someone tightly pinched my back and I turned.

"Oops, very sorry. Very very sorry, I thought you were someone…" the girl who pinched me said in a sweet voice.

I didn't reply. I couldn't. I had never seen someone so beautiful in my life. I could hardly pay attention to what she was saying now. All of a sudden, I started to respect God's artistic works even more. I mean, He had already set the bar high with Kanika, but this lady's beauty was what could be called a *recherché*. She was a combination of Aishwarya Rai and Jennifer Lawrence. Her body was by far the most perfect thing made by God ever. At the same time, her face had the innocence of a child.

"It's okay, it's okay. No problem. My pleasure. I think we should do it again sometime. Thank you," I blabbered after I received one more pinch, this time from Saurabh. Obviously she gave me a look as if I was deranged and left.

"What were you doing there? Are you out of your mind?" Sanjana asked.

"I think I am in love with her," I said and rushed straight towards Akshay to ask about her. She was his childhood school friend Namrata, and to my surprise, she had recently moved to Ahmedabad. Akshay also told me she was single and I could ask her out if I wished to.

The Tomatina festival began soon after, and as we entered the tomato pool. I was pretty sure Namrata was the only goal in my life after I saw her in a wet, white t-shirt and red shorts.

The next event was the Tilak – a ritual in a hindu wedding where the bride's father puts some vermilion on the groom's forehead and all the other elders of the family bless him. With the changing trend, the Tilak is followed by Sangeet where members of both the families and friends dance to celebrate the occasion. We reached the destination and headed straight to the open bar and had a few drinks. After a while, I saw Namrata getting on the stage with a few girls. She must have been backstage all this while and that's why I had not spotted her. She began dancing, and she did it gracefully. Dressed in a neon-green coloured sari and dupatta, a sleeveless blouse with beads of different colours on it, and open hair – she seemed to have broken her own record in the beauty department. Now the first two positions for the most beautiful women I had ever seen belonged to her.

"Hey!"

"Oh hi!" I said as I realized it was Namrata. I had come to get a drink for Sanjana and myself. The Bollywood night was in progress and the young crowd was high and dancing their asses off. I was surprised to see her come up to me to say hi.

"Suhaan, right?" she inquired. *Wow, she knows my name. Maybe she enquired about me from Akshay like I did. Is she interested in me?*

"Yes, err, I am sorry but have we met before?" I asked. *Way to go Suhaan. Act all jazzy and cool in front of a girl who could use guys like you as litter bins.*

"In fact we have. Remember the pinching incident which happened earlier today at the carnival? I am the same girl, Namrata."

"Oh yeah, right. I am sorry but I am really bad with remembering people." *Somebody please kill me. I am not this stupid. This is a new low even for me. I do not deserve to live.*

"Oh is it! You must be having some memory loss up there in your head because after getting out all my details from Akshay, and searching for me all evening and ogling at me while I was performing, you still don't remember me!"

I felt like I was standing naked and she was staring at me. The embarrassment was indefinable. She was watching me all along and knew how interested I was in her. I didn't know what to say. I was almost choked.

"Oops! Err, there's no escaping women, is there?" I said running my hand through my hair.

"You should look at your face! Chill, it's okay. Anyway, let's start again. I am Namrata," she said putting out her hand for a handshake.

"Hi, I am Suhaan and I am sorry for being a total jerk. I very well remember your name, address, your qualifications, and what not. The only thing which I don't have is your phone number which I plan to have by the end of this wedding. I've literally checked each and every one of your post and photos on your Facebook profile and trust me, someone like you should most certainly not keep their profile so easily accessible."

"You are sweet. Let's take a walk around the place?" she said as we started taking a stroll. It was getting colder every few minutes and to my surprise, Namrata didn't seem to be feeling one bit cold in her sleeveless blouse. I always wonder how that is possible with women.

We talked about everything. I told her everything about myself – from my school days, to my obsession with cricket, to dating Kanika. She gasped when I told her about how long we had been together. Her longest run with a guy had been three months. She also reciprocated well and told me everything about herself. She told me how she hated it when her father had to keep making business trips. They even had to shift to entirely new cities regularly – the most recent being Ahmedabad, because of the nature of his work.

The next day, after the *tel-baan* ritual – where both the families apply turmeric, oil and a few other things to the bride and groom – we went to our rooms to get ready for the Punjabi themed lunch at the Gulmohar Garden. We were all dressed up in our Punjabi kurtas and pathanis and wore a *kada* on one of our hands. The girls were looking cute in their suits and kurtis with their hair tied up with *parandas*. Once again, Namrata looked her best, surpassing all the other lovely looking ladies fair and square.

> *"Dil karda ae tere kol aake ruk java,*
> *Teri bukkal vich rakh k sir muk java,*
> *Hanju ban k digga teriya akkhan da*
> *Tere bulla de kol aake sukh java…"*

I narrated a short verse in Punjabi when she came and stood next to our group. It meant: (My heart wishes I could come near you and stay forever, that I could die with my head on your lap, I wish I could fall from your eyes like a tear, and stop near your lips forever.)

"Waah waah!" All the friends said in unison except for Saurabh who was a bit taken aback, and Namrata, who blushed.

The garden was full of gulmohar trees and hence the name. They had put up a *lassi* stall and a stall named *'Desi daaru ka theka'* which meant Indian liquor, though it was serving the finest liquor from across the world. There were also a few food stalls offering north Indian delicacies. They had also put up a few charpoys – single beds made of tightly knit ropes around its wooden legs, mostly used in villages. It was another fun-filled event and once again, we danced our way through it. Namrata and I did steal our moments together with the constant gazing and occasional running into each other which was more purposeful than by chance.

"Hey, want to sit on the swing hanging by that tree?" I asked her.

She happily obliged and we had a wonderful time alone. I had never felt this way before. Two years with Kanika and I don't think I had shared so much with her.

"Namrata, let's go or else we'll be late for the baraat!" her friend shouted.

"Yeah coming!" she said and went off hurriedly after giving me a smile.

It was evening and the baraat was ready to leave from the entrance of Sitara Hotel towards Mughal Garden, a multi-storey beautiful garden where Mehr's family was waiting to welcome the baraatis. We all were pumped up as the joy of dancing on the streets in an Indian baraat is incomparable. After an hour of dancing to desi beats, we finally reached the destination. The entrance reminded me of the movie *Troy* with its huge gates, above which soldiers were ready to defend the city with their weapons. This was almost similar, except for its Mughal architecture with corridors and huge windows above the gate. It was a grand reception and the varmala ceremony was the best I had ever seen. Even a fatty like Akshay was looking like a prince standing in the balcony on the first floor with Mehr beside him. We were all watching it from the garden and it was something fantabulous.

Akshay and Mehr then proceeded to perform their wedding rituals and we all went to the top floor of the garden to enjoy some Sufi music.

"It's not that I don't believe in a serious relationship, it's just that I haven't met the right guy yet. Every time I find someone with whom I feel I can get serious, the guy turns out to be a jerk or I suddenly start losing interest. I know it's a bit weird, but that's how I..." she paused and gave me a puzzled look.

I was gazing at her in astonishment. I could not get over her amazing looks. We were walking on one of the deserted streets of Ramoji outside the Mughal Garden as we were more interested in listening to each other's voices than the Sufi maestro.

"Is something wrong, Suha..." she started but I leaned towards her and kissed her. The little hesitance vanished when a second later, she kissed me back. Suddenly, she held my hand and pulled me towards the garden to find a car. Within a few minutes, we were at the reception of Sitara Hotel.

Hey, I have some company, please bunk in Raju's room for tonight.

I texted Saurabh.

The next thirty minutes were the most amazing ones of my life. We were lying naked on the bed of my room, wondering what had just happened. I was chuffed to bits and didn't know the bounds of my joy. It was just the previous day that I could hardly imagine befriending her, and here I was, lying naked on the bed with her after having the most wonderful sex of my life. God couldn't be more kind, I thought and slept.

"It was a nice re-union guys, I am glad we got a chance to meet," I said.

We were getting ready to leave for our homes the next morning after the memorable two days.

"Oh shut up you bastard, as if you were even there to spend time with us," Sanjana said. After some more scolding and sulking, the fellows finally forgave me.

Namrata was getting similar responses while parting from her friends. Unfortunately, we both were on different flights and were ruing the fact even though we had made plans to meet the very next day in Ahmedabad!

Namrata and I had been dating for almost six months. Life couldn't be any better even if it tried its best. On the one hand I was dating an amazing girl like her and on the other, I was playing good cricket for the club. The big news was that I had been shortlisted for the Gujarat Ranji team squad. My parents were patient enough to give it time as long as I saw hope of making it big.

"I must say I am amazed, Suhaan. I've never seen you like this before," Saurabh said while we were video chatting on Skype.

"I agree. This is new for me. But Namrata is different, bro. I've never felt so strongly for anyone ever before. I think she is the one," I said.

"Well, you do seem pretty sure about her. You've even told your parents about her. So when are you thinking of proposing to her?" Saurabh inquired.

"Tonight. I just hope she agrees to marry me," I replied. I had talked to him a few times about Namrata. I was jumping to go and propose to her all the time, but Saurabh had calmed me down and asked me to give it some more time. But today, even he was convinced.

"She sure will, man. What possible reason could she have to say no? Just go for it," Saurabh motivated me.

"Hey baby, what's up?" Namrata said as soon as she received the call. I had called up to ask her to meet me.

"Nothing much, just wanted to ask if we could make plans for tonight."

"Naughty plans or just plans plans?" she giggled. Finding places to make out had become the order of our meetings recently, with the most common being finding deserted streets and doing it in my car.

"Just plans baby. I was thinking we could go for a nice dinner or something."

"Sure, works for me. See you at eight."

I made reservations in Tinello, her favourite restaurant at the Hyatt Regency. I decided to take my dad's BMW. Presentation always matters, I thought, and hence booked the entire restaurant for the evening. I took a bath, dressed in my best, left home at 7:40 p.m. and reached her bungalow exactly at eight.

Hey, I am outside. Come quickly. I texted her.

"Are you serious? It's only eight! I was just going to begin getting dressed," she called up and said.

"Eight was the time, wasn't it?"

"Yes, but when have you ever come on time before? How am I supposed to know you'll be on time today?" she said. She was right. I had never been on time before.

"Haha! Relax baby, take your own time. I'll run a couple of errands in the meantime. Let me know when you're ready and I'll be back," I said.

I didn't have any errands to run. Even if I did, I wasn't in a state of mind to think about them. I decided to just park outside her society and wait.

"Hi baby, really sorry to keep you waiting for so long," she said kissing my left cheek while getting seated in the car, after making me wait for forty-five long minutes. She was looking resplendent in a black dress.

It was a fifteen minute drive from her place to the hotel. As soon as we reached the restaurant, she found it weird that an otherwise occupied restaurant was empty, quite literally. Moreover, the place was lit up beautifully with candles. All the tables were cornered to the walls except for one in the centre which was reserved for us.

"Okay, what's going on, Suhaan?" she asked.

"Well, I thought it's nice to bring up such surprises at times to keep the spark alive in a relationship."

"Oh God! You're sounding like an eighty year old. It's only been six months and this fellow has to take efforts to 'keep the spark alive,'" she mocked me. I really must have sounded stupid.

"Shall we order?" I asked after we got seated. She nodded.

After having a lovely dinner, I thought it was finally the right time to pop the question.

"What is this, Suhaan?" she asked surprised. I took out a small diary from the pocket of my blazer and handed it to her. It was a small photo album with our photos in it. Each photo had a movie title, printed on the top as similar to the situation when the photo was clicked. The first photo was from Akshay and Mehr's wedding where she was sitting on the swing and I was standing behind her. The photo was titled *Jab We Met*, a popular Kareena and Shahid Kapoor movie. The next was both of us soaked wet in rain after having onion bhajias in Mount Abu. Our long drive kept getting longer and we reached Mount Abu from Ahmedabad without any prior plans. It was titled *Zindagi Na Milegi Dobara* as she had been reluctant all the way and I had given her a lecture about living life to the fullest. I had managed to assemble a few more pictures and had given them titles before we reached the final page which was blank with *Mujhse Shaadi Karogi?* written in the centre in large fonts. This was the moment. I had almost wet my pants. I was waiting for a reaction. Namrata, who was otherwise smiling till now, became serious.

"Namrata?" I called out, dying for a reply.

"Suhaan, I don't know what to say. All this is so beautiful, so perfect. But, I can't marry you, Suhaan," she said. For a moment, I felt as if my ears weren't receiving the right messages. For a second, my heart was heavy, sad, and broken at the same time. I sat there with a blank face for a while, but after a few seconds, I asked her the reason for saying no.

"Trust me when I say this, baby, I was thinking about it since a couple of weeks and was planning to bring it up very soon. The thing is, I've started to really like you. Maybe I am falling deeply in love with you, and I do not wish to get more involved because it may affect both of us."

"I can't understand what you're saying, Namrata. What is the problem if you love me?" I was shocked.

"Hear me out first, Suhaan. You told me a couple of weeks ago that you might get a call to play in the Ranji Trophy tournament very soon, and if you do, you'll have to travel a lot. Moreover, if you someday manage to make it big and reach the international level, the amount of travelling will only increase. All my life my mother and I have had complaints about my father. He was hardly around due to his work. He has hardly been there on any of my birthdays, anniversaries, and sometimes in situations where we have really needed him by our side. I've made a compromise in my father's case, but I am not ready to let it happen with me again."

"Wow, I didn't see that coming," I said while resting my back on the chair and looking around the restaurant thinking about what had just happened.

"I am sorry, Suhaan, but you have to understand it's for our good. It is very difficult for me too," Namrata said trying to console me, not that it was making any difference.

"Hey, you could travel with me. That shouldn't be a problem."

"Be practical Suhaan. What about my life and my career? I can't live a life packed in a suitcase and keep wandering from one place to another doing nothing."

Unfortunately for me, all of what she was saying made sense. Things were going good in the cricket field for me and I was really optimistic. Going on with the relationship would have only resulted in both of us getting hurt. Dejected, I had to agree with her and we had a quiet drive back to her home. She cried, and cried a lot which made one thing very clear. It was very difficult for her too. I had always taken life as it came to me and never gave a thought to anything seriously. Namrata also just happened in my life and I carried on without thinking about the future. I knew I was falling in love with her with each passing day but still did not take it seriously and I was regretting it. The only thing which I chose to do with so much enthusiasm was now coming in between me and the girl of my dreams. Finally, we parted ways and made false promises of staying in touch.

It was three in the morning when Namrata's phone rang.

"Suhaan! Is everything okay? Why are you calling at this time? Where are you?" she posted a flurry of questions before I could answer.

"Everything is wonderful. I am calling at this time because I have something important to tell you. I am right outside your bungalow, so please come down right now!"

"What! Oh my god! What are you doing here? Somebody will see you! Please go now, I promise I'll meet you in the morning," she said while peeping out of the window.

"I cannot wait till morning. Either you come down and allow me to talk to you or I am ringing your doorbell and then I'll have to talk to your parents."

"You are crazy. Wait there and don't make any noise," she whispered after hanging up.

"Okay listen, I've thought about it all evening and I've decided I am going to join dad's business and stop playing cricket. That way, I won't have to travel anywhere and we'll be able to stay with each other all the time," I said.

"No way! You are not doing that. The last thing I want to do is be a hurdle between you and your dreams."

"You are not a hurdle, trust me. I have given it a lot of thought and I am pretty clear about what I am doing. I love you, Namrata, and I love you like crazy. I have never felt so sure about anything ever in my life. At the restaurant, you gave all those reasons and I couldn't handle it at that moment and agreed. But the fact is that I need you more than anything in my life. You are all that I want. The moment we parted our ways, I felt a sense of emptiness, a moment where my life seemed to be meaningless, and I can't tell you how horrible it was. I can't let you go baby. I just can't."

"I don't know what to say, but it doesn't seem right on my part. It feels like I am stealing your happiness. It'll be very selfish. No Suhaan, I don't think it's right."

"*You* are my happiness! Not some bat and ball game. I have talked to Mom, Dad and Saurabh and they all are with me on this. Can't I make such a small sacrifice for the love of my life?" I tried to explain to her and after a rally of few more questions and answers, she finally agreed.

"You don't have a clue how the last few hours have been for me. Moments have felt like ages. I love you baby," she said after hugging me tightly and kissing me.

"Of all the things about you, this is what I missed the most," I joked caressing her lips.

The next day, Namrata's parents were taken into confidence and fortunately everything went smoothly. Apparently, the fathers had met each other once or twice in business conclaves and luckily had heard good things about each other. Namrata's parents wanted a grand wedding as she was their only child and my parents happily agreed as I was the apple of their eyes too. On the other hand, Bose da was disappointed after knowing about my plans and he had the right to be so. He had literally taken me under his guidance and groomed me all this while. Explaining the situation to him were the toughest twenty-five minutes of my life. A few months later, we got married at the Taj Lake Palace, Udaipur.

During our courtship, I had joined the business and was trying to take a keen interest in it, but it hadn't been able to win my love yet. The construction business can be marked as one of the more passive lines of work a man can do. All the construction part was taken care of by the contractors and supervisors, and apart from the occasional inspections, we didn't have much to do. The purchase department was good enough in its job. The only thing we had to focus upon was sales, which meant sitting in the office all day like couch potatoes and dealing with whatever customers the middle-men would bring.

Contrary to what I had thought, I did miss playing cricket. Very often, I would see small kids playing on the streets and older ones going for the big hits on the grounds and wonder if I could still somehow continue, but then one call or text from Namrata would take that thought away.

It had just been a couple of months since we had returned from Australia after a nice honeymoon. Namrata's presence in my house had worked like a charm for my family, whereas for me the charm of a newly wedded couple was already fizzing out. She was blossoming more than ever before; my parents loved her and she loved them back. They were a happy bunch of people. I, on the contrary, was slowly turning out to be only a shadow of my fun-loving, devil may care attitude self. The old Suhaan was dying. Though slowly, but steadily, I was becoming more serious and was forgetting what living and enjoying life was all about. I knew that I was at fault not knowing what had changed.

"Hey there's this new movie which released this Friday and it has my favourite actor in it. Let's go for it tonight," Namrata said as soon as I entered the room after getting back from office.

"I am a bit tired, baby. It was a hectic day. Please ask one of your friends," I said removing my shirt and sprawling on the bed.

I wasn't really all that tired but was irritated. It had been so many months and I wasn't enjoying the business one bit. I was pushing myself all this time, thinking it was something very new for me and I'd take time to adjust to this routine. I had even expressed my boredom, lack of interest to Dad and even he had explained that I was entering a new phase in my life and I'd have to be patient to accept this change. But now, I was beginning to lose it.

"Suhaan, this is the fifth time you're refusing to go out with me in two months. You don't seem to be like the person I loved anymore. You hardly take me out now and it seems you've forgotten how to smile. How on earth am I supposed to live this way?" she whined.

"It's nothing like that. Just that the work is a bit hectic these days and nothing more," I lied.

"Even Dad works with you for the entire day, but he always seems to be happy and energetic. I don't understand how you get so tired."

"You're talking like a child. I do all the running around. From site inspections to purchase orders to dealing with customers – everything's upon me now. You'll have to understand."

"Okay, you freshen up. I'll ask Ramu kaka to get the dinner table ready," she said with a sad face after sighing.

The same story continued in spite of Namrata's constant efforts to woo me and 'keep the spark alive' in our relationship. Yes, this time the situation was dire enough that we had to work hard to show we loved and cared for each other. Slowly, she started losing her patience and the discussions which mostly consisted of me whining and she sometimes trying to cheer me up and at the others apologizing for no mistake of hers, started taking the shape of ugly quarrels.

"Why did you do this to me, Suhaan? Why? Why did you marry me and spoil everything?" she said while sobbing continuously. It was another one of those horrible nights where instead of cozying up to each other, we were finding reasons for our miserably failing marriage. She was sitting on the sofa near the bed.

"I didn't do anything purposely and you know that. Stop being the scapegoat for no reason and try to act maturely. Things change after people get married. We are not kids anymore who can fool around all day with no sense of responsibility," I answered back irritated, getting up from the chair at the small office table where I was busy with my phone.

"Oh, is it? Then what do matured people do? Is fighting every night a sign of being matured? Is having no sex, no intimacy at all towards each other a sign? Is it a sign of maturity that you hate coming home after work every night? I simply rue the fact that after such a lovely time with Mom and Dad at the dinner table I have to come into the bedroom and be with someone like you for the next few hours. You either act like I simply don't exist or my existence has become so much of a problem to you that you can't bear staying in the same room with me."

"I don't know if I can keep catering to your stupid complaints anymore. Since the day we got married, all you have done is complain. In fact, you started changing since the day we got engaged. Either I have to do things your way or not do them at all. In this room, I can't even watch a cricket match if I wish to. I sacrificed so much for you. I gave up playing cricket just for you, and this is how you're paying me back. You never cared enough for my sacrifices for you. Being selfish is all that you've done," I said raising my voice a bit.

"I can't believe you just said that, Suhaan. I just can't believe it. Did I ask you to leave cricket? In fact, I was the one who broke up with you in the first place so that I don't come between your ambitions. It was you who forced me to accept your proposal by telling me that cricket meant nothing to you when you compared it to me. You know what Suhaan, the reason that we are in this situation today is because you could never let cricket get out of you. I am pretty sure you think I am the reason for you sitting in that packed office all day and living a life which you are least interested in. Every time you see a cricket match, you feel anger, a state of despair and hatred towards me which results in you behaving this way with me. You are okay with Mom, Dad and even the watchman, the gardener and Ramu kaka in this house, but not me. You are the one who is selfish, Suhaan. You don't think about the pain I am going through since we got married. All you think about is your troubles, your sacrifices, your pain and noth...."

"*Aargh!*"

I shouted and punched the TV screen with all the force I could execute and it shattered into pieces. I could not take it anymore and all my pent up anger had resulted in what I did. Namrata was petrified. She didn't move an inch and was just staring at me in shock.

"Suhaan, is everything okay? What was that noise?" Mom and Dad were knocking on the door a minute later. The noise was loud enough to cross the walls and reach the nearby rooms.

"Err, nothing, Mom. A vase fell down and broke. We'll clean it up. You guys go and sleep," I lied to keep them away from this mess. My hand was bleeding like water dripping from a leaked hose pipe.

"Open the door, Suhaan. Where is Namrata? I want to see her," Mom said in a tense voice.

Namrata ran and opened the door.

"Oh my God! What is going on here? What happened? Why is your hand bleeding, Suhaan? Why is Namrata crying?"

Namrata hugged my mother tightly as soon as she entered. Dad ran outside to get some first aid while Mom pacified Namrata.

The secret was out now. The only thing with which we both agreed in the few months of our marriage was to not let our parents get to know about our problems. Though I sensed that Dad noticed the changes in my personality, but probably thought it was because of work.

"Now would anyone please explain what the heck is going on here?" Dad asked after he finished dressing my fist.

"I can't stay here anymore, Ma. I want a divorce," Namrata said. All of us were shocked.

"Why? What are you saying, Beta? At least tell me what has happened," Mom said.

Namrata then explained everything to them. She told them how I had changed since our engagement and how much leaving cricket had affected me. She told them everything about how our relationship had never seen an upside since our wedding day. Even I listened to her carefully and didn't object because all of it was true.

"Where are you going, Namrata? Do you want something?" Mom asked as Namrata started going out of the room, but she didn't answer.

"Rajveer, come quickly. Namrata is going out of the main gate!"

Dad rushed out as soon as he heard Mom calling him. I stood there undecided about what to do. There was too much going on inside my head at the moment.

When the three of them didn't return after quite some time, I called up Mom and asked her if they were okay. Mom told me that Namrata wanted to go to her parents' place and they were taking her there. I could see my marriage falling apart and I didn't know what to do. They dropped her and came back very late.

The next day, both sets of parents tried to understand the situation and tried to mend the differences. Namrata was sure of her feelings but I couldn't decide what I wanted. I loved her like anything, was crazy about her, and it wasn't as if I hadn't tried to save our relationship. I just wasn't able to. I still tried and talked to Namrata to give it one final chance, but she knew there was no future for us together. Her parents were furious with me. I was threatened with everything, from dragging me to the court to not forgiving me, but it was Namrata who didn't want things to take an ugly turn. A few days later, I received the divorce papers at my office.

I was all alone. The separation with Namrata had done more bad to me rather than good as I had thought. I used to spend my days sitting in one of the corner offices, cancelling all my meetings and asking the mangers to take calls on important issues. I had lost track of time completely and my life was going nowhere.

A couple of months passed in the same fashion and Mom was really worried about me. Even Dad was getting more worried day by day and decided to talk to me.

"How long is it going to be this way, Suhaan? It's like you have stopped living. You have gone into a shell and refuse to come out, no matter what," Dad said.

"I am alright, Dad. Everything's fine. It's just that I need some time to come out of it." I explained.

"And how do you think that will happen? Go Suhaan, move out. It's not the end of your life. It's a beautiful world out there waiting for you to soak in the pleasures it has to offer. Your staying this way has affected your mother's health as well. She is depressed. It's like I am living with two dead people. You have to give yourself another chance, my son. If not for yourself, do it for your mother," Dad reproached.

"But what do I do, Dad? It seems like I have lost that essence in life. I am not able to concentrate on anything."

"Try and meet some girls. Have a few casual affairs. All in all, just let go. It won't harm you to start smiling again."

"No, Dad, I do not want to meet anyone. My heart is too vulnerable at this moment for that."

"Start playing cricket then. That's the only thing which can make you smile again I suppose," Dad advised.

"That's impossible, Dad. It's too late now. I don't think there is much scope for me after staying out of the scene for so long. I haven't played for almost a year and I think I must have lost my rhythm. Budding cricketers hardly get a chance once, and in my case I had a reference from Bose da and let him down. I don't think they'll take me."

"Why don't you let Bose da decide that? Just give him a call and see how it goes. We know it won't be very romantic, but who knows if you're lucky and he is in a good mood, you might have a shot!" he motivated me.

I felt a sense of rejuvenation after talking to Dad. I decided I'd not let my life get wasted. I'd give it a try for myself and Mom's sake. The next morning, I called Coach Shubendhu Bose.

"Woah! Look who is calling!" Bose da exclaimed.

"Hello Sir, how are you?" I asked.

"Well, I am good but surely could be better if the players whom I bank upon stopped dumping me," he said taking a jibe at me. He had really been working hard putting around a good word for me and telling people I would be the find of the season.

"Oh come on Bose da, you've already made me apologize a lot for it. Spare me now."

"Anyway, tell me what made you call me? And how is Namrata?" he asked and then I told him about the past year. I also told him the reason why I had called him.

"I am very sorry to hear that, Suhaan. It must be a really hard time for you. About you wanting to play cricket again, I'll see what I can do, but you'll have to promise me that there won't be any quitting this time."

I promised to take it up more seriously than ever before and not let him down this time. Once again, I started playing with the GCA Club House. The first few days were tough and I was struggling to get my rhythm back, but Bose da and the other coaches were immensely supportive.

Keeping in mind my club level performances and the reputation that Bose da had in the organization, a couple of months later, he got my name shortlisted for the Gujarat Ranji Trophy team. I have to admit I was really blessed to know someone like Bose da personally to get a second chance. Otherwise even good players like me sometimes had to work day-in and day-out to play club level in this country.

Gujarat had never won the Ranji Trophy. Like every year, the hopes weren't too high this time either.

As expected, we started our campaign on a low as we lost to a strong Rajasthan side by 189 runs. Jaimin Patel, the medium pacer was particularly ridiculed for his forgettable bowling figures of 30-0-131-0. Fortuitously, Jaimin's loss was my gain as I was warming the bench in that game and got to play in my first Ranji match against the strongest side of all time, Mumbai. I had decided I would not let my coach down. The pitch was a bowler's paradise and I bowled with all the pace and control that I could. I single-handedly devastated the Mumbai batting line up and picked up 7 wickets. They were all out for a paltry total of 126. My bowling figures were an impressive 14.3-4-21-7. We won the match comprehensively to the surprise of one and all.

Our next match was with an in-form Karnataka side who could say they had eleven players playing their top game at the same time. They were the defending champions and players like Robin Uthhapa, Manish Pandey, and the captain Vinay Kumar among others were replicating their previous year's performance with ease. They won the toss and chose to bat first and put up a big score of 417/10. In response, our batsmen faltered and made silly mistakes to give their wickets away. We were 200-7 when I came to bat. Even after my known batting skills, the team management didn't want to disturb the batting order for a new player. It was my turn to flaunt my batting skills now. I played with caution and after settling in, hit the bowlers all around the ground to show everybody I could bat as well. Navroz Daruwala, the wicketkeeper-batsman of our team gave me good support. We put up 214 runs for the 8th wicket before I gave up my wicket when I was at 91 runs. By the end of the innings, the team's score was 449 and we had achieved the much needed first innings lead. I had managed to impress one and all fortunately. The match ended in a draw. This led to a flurry of stupendous batting and bowling performances by me which even gave the team new hope that they could put up a good show and make a statement. Sohail Khan, another pace bowler also bowled with rhythm and we both began hunting for wickets in pairs in all our future games.

We lost to Mumbai in the semi-finals but the message was clear that nobody could take Gujarat lightly anymore and I had announced my arrival in style as I ended up being the highest wicket-taker.

A few days later, Bose da visited my place and gave me some exciting news.

"The IPL auctions are coming up. Let's sell you!" Bose da joked.

"Man, IPL! Bose da you don't know my love for the IPL. Since the day it has started, I have been dreaming to play in that league someday, be it for any team. The glitz, the glamour, the fun quotient – everything is perfect about it," I exclaimed.

"Well, then let's get down to business. The buzz is around that you'll be the hot cake this season. even though the team owners lust for big names and foreign players. There are many coaches and support staff with the Ranji teams which are directly associated with their respective states' IPL teams and get their players bought, be it for minimum wages. Gujarat doesn't have an IPL team of its own and that could be a little bit of a drawback for you. Hence, I'd suggest you enter the auction with the minimum base price of ten lakhs to be on the safer side."

"Too less Bose da, let the price be a crore," I said.

"What? You don't want to play the IPL, is it? Who'll give that price for an uncapped player?" Bose da remonstrated.

"I haven't performed so well at the Ranji for nothing, Sir. I am least interested in the money. I just want to grab some eyeballs."

"You've gone insane. You'll be in the news for being a fool. Playing in the IPL and performing well there can give your international career a jump of at least three years. But for that you'll have to be in some team in the first place. Moreover, this is the year when fresh auctions will take place which means all the teams will release a majority of their players and will be eager to buy them back from the auctions."

"Okay, if you're insisting so much, we can keep it down to fifty lakhs. Not a penny less."

"So be it," Bose da finally gave in to my stubbornness.

I was sitting in front of the TV since 8:30 a.m. on the auction day. One could spot all the big shots dressed up in their crisply ironed suits, neatly combed and gelled up hair ready to spend their enormous amounts of money to buy players. Kids in normal households bought videogames worth a few thousands, whereas these corporate honchos bought IPL teams worth a few hundred crores. Mr Mallya, the owner of the RCB was dressed in a white shirt and black trousers. He also sported a ponytail, so was definitely a bit of a fashionista.

There was the Ambani mother and son duo, owners of one of the most star studded teams, MI. Their team had received great adulation, irrespective of home games or away because of the presence of Sachin Tendulkar. For Mrs Ambani, this could just be like going to a kitty party and spending some money on drinks and a card game; they were that rich.

Amongst the others, there were members representing the GMR group, owners of the Delhi franchise; coach Stephen Fleming and others from CSK; a few less popular faces from superstar Mr Khan's team the KKR; the street smart selectors of RR, who had a knack of picking up lesser known but excellent players for less money; the experienced management team of the Hyderabad team consisting of former greats like VVS Laxman, Kris Srikanth and coach Tom Moody.

And then, there was the Punjab regime, and with them, was the beautiful Ashlesha Kapoor, co-owner of the Punjab franchise. She was the twenty-six-year-old, daughter of a celebrated Bollywood director-producer and had a dream debut a couple of years ago. I had a big time crush on her even before she had started her acting career and was spotted in parties with her father.

Vishal, the TV anchor, got busy welcoming and taking everyone's views outside the auction hall.

"Hello and welcome to the big day that everyone has been talking about. This year we bring to you the grand auctions as the team managements this year have the right to retain up to a maximum of four players only and let everyone else go. A lot of planning has been done by all the selectors and they have all come up with a few expected, but also a few shocking retentions and releases. There is a plethora of players to go up for sale today which includes some very big names as well. So let's get on with the show and get some insights from the panel of the teams' selectors," Vishal said and started interviewing a few celebrities and officials while they entered the hall.

Everyone had a few players in their minds which they wanted at any cost, literally. The IPL had seen some surprises every year at the auctions and this year was expected to be no different. Destiny sometimes had been a bit harsh on the teams. When KKR released Chris Gayle as he wasn't performing, he was bought by RCB the next year and had smashed a century in his first match. To add salt to KKR's wounds, it was in a match against them and Gayle had been a revelation thereafter. Similarly, MI bought Glenn Maxwell for around a million dollars, gave him just a single game in the entire season and released him. Ashlesha's Punjab grabbed him with both arms and the 'Big Show', as he is popularly known, became the talking point in opposition team meetings all of a sudden.

"We have been talking about all the big guns going under the hammer throughout, but there is this one uncapped all rounder from the Gujarat Ranji team who has surprised one and all by quoting a base price of fifty lakhs! Experts are saying he was the reason why Gujarat, being a much weaker team, went till the semi-finals this year. Still, fifty lakhs seems a bit farfetched to me. The lad must have had some real confidence in himself to quote that kind of a price. Anyway, time will tell what destiny has in store for him. All the owners are in the hall now and it looks like we are ready to begin the rigmarole. We shall now move on to the auction where Mr John will take over the proceedings. Enjoy!" Vishal concluded.

"Farfetched my ass," I said with a wry smile sitting in front of the TV.

The auction hall was very elegant. It had two big entrance gates made of rich polished wood. Someone as delicate as Ashlesha would need both hands to push it with all her strength to open it. The hall was big enough to get all the teams' round tables, fit in a few camera persons, and a dais for the dignitaries. The round tables for the teams were placed in a zig-zag manner, with CSK taking the first table near the gate. Diagonally in front of them were DD, and diagonally behind DD on the other side were KKR, then RCB, SRH and so on. KXIP were allotted the table near the second gate. They were at the same table every year. It was as if they asked for it.

Six feet tall, fair, broad shoulders, nice built, John himself looked like more of a sportsman. The only thing which was a letdown in his otherwise good looks was a pair of glasses which were in fashion twenty-five years ago!

"Good evening and a warm welcome to everybody. I will quickly go through the regulations before we begin the auctions."

And he went on to give all the details. After that, he called the IPL secretary Mr Biswal to hand him over the badge with a player's name on it. Mr Biswal obliged by getting up and moving towards the lady standing on the dais behind John holding the bag which contained all the badges and handed over one to John after pulling one out.

"So the first player to go up for sale today is the South African opening batsman Hashim Amla and he is priced at a hundred lakhs."

He started the proceedings like he was a purveyor of luxury paintings.

He waited for a few seconds and then carried on.

"Do I have a hundred lakhs for him?"

On seeing no one interested, he declared Amla unsold.

Amla is such a legend in Test and ODI cricket and there are no takers for him in the IPL. Such a strange game cricket has become with these different formats!

John would request a dignitary to give him a badge every time to choose the next player up for sale.

"Thank you, sir. The next player up for sale is the Indian all-rounder Yuvraj Singh, who was the most expensive player last year, and his base price is a hundred and fifty lakhs. Do I have my first bid?"

As soon as John read out Yuvraj Singh's name, one could see members murmuring at various tables. No one had expected his name to come up so soon. Most certainly, a bidding war was coming up. Yuvi had had a decent outing last year with the RCB and still they had released him, maybe to get him back at a lesser price. It was yet to be seen how this strategy worked out for them.

CSK were the first to go. Their coach Stephen Fleming raised the baton which was given to each team for signaling their bid.

"A hundred and fifty from CSK."

Immediately SRH went up.

"A hundred and eighty, Sunrisers."

"Two hundred, CSK."

It went on for a while before a few new bidders joined in.

"Four hundred and fifty lakhs from KXIP."

"Four hundred and eighty, RCB."

"Six hundred, MI."

Each and every team had bid for him at least once, except Delhi. They were sitting quietly and observing the bid rise quickly like mercury in a thermometer on a hot summer's day. The bid had already crossed a whopping thousand lakhs! Some of the teams had already backed out. And the last bid was RCB's. There was half a smile on the owners' faces as they were happy their plan had worked out. But just then, DD came in.

"Eleven hundred lakhs from DD."

RCB would still not back out.

"Twelve hundred lakhs, RCB."

"Thirteen hundred lakhs, DD."

DD raised the bet immediately.

"Fourteen hundred lakhs, RCB."

Again, there was silence. DD hadn't backed out though. And all of a sudden, the Ambani scion Rahul representing MI raised the baton.

"The Mumbai Indians have joined the race again. Fifteen hundred lakhs, MI."

"Sixteen hundred lakhs, DD. Do I have seventeen hundred lakhs?"

But this time it seemed like it was all over. Both MI and RCB had signaled they were out and John waited for a few seconds before declaring Yuvraj Singh sold to DD for a crazy sum of sixteen hundred lakhs. May be being out of the national side was proving to be a blessing for him after all.

The auction continued with a sea of players going under the hammer. It was the nature of the IPL to spring some surprises and it lived up to it this year as well, quite vehemently.

Now it was the turn for the uncapped players. There were many players who had done extremely well during the domestic season. The IPL format required that the playing XI of any team cannot have more than four international players. This gave the new chaps a real chance to prove their mettle. My name was on the list and I was sweating it out in front of the TV now as the uncapped players were about to go for sale. I knew it very well that there were a few fierce competitors against me in the domestic circuit who could shatter my dreams. Such a high base price could backfire.

The auction continued and the uncapped players were being picked up by the teams for peanuts like they were buying vegetables. Most of them had ten lakhs as their base price. I was feeling the heat already. The only respite was Mumbai right arm fast bowler Manik Salve being picked up by MI for a hundred and twenty lakhs.

And finally, it was my turn. John read out my name aloud.

"And the next player is Suhaan Arora from Gujarat, and his base price is, well that's something unusual – fifty lakhs." John paused and read out the base price.

There were no biddings. My hopes were sinking with each passing second. The decision to quote a high base price and raise people's eyebrows were now doing the same to me. I was beginning to feel what a stupid decision it was. There were a few murmurs around, but no one was looking like they were interested in bidding. My prayers had begun already. I feared the look on Bose da's face.

"Do I have fifty lakhs for the ambitious lad?" John enquired, and soon as he was about to declare me unsold, Ashlesha raised the baton.

"Fifty lakhs! The first bid has come in. Do I have sixty?"

Immediately, CSK looked interested and they joined.

"Seventy lakhs, CSK."

And then something unusual started happening. At least three or four other teams started bidding for me at the same instant. The bid had already reached a whopping two hundred lakhs! It was as if they were all playing the waiting game and planning to get me at my base price, but as soon as one of them bid, they all pounced. CSK and KXIP; were looking extremely interested in having me on board as it looked like they were keeping the baton down after making one bid just because the rule asked them to.

On the other side of the TV, I was grinning from ear to ear as even I hadn't expected such a response. I couldn't decide if I wanted to play for CSK or KXIP, the former had India's best captain ever leading the team whereas the latter had Ashlesha, whom I had adored for years. Plus, KXIP was in great form last year.

"Two hundred and twenty lakhs, RCB," John continued.

SRH, MI, KKR, RR and DD had all made one bid each and backed out. There were only three teams in the race now.

"Two hundred and fifty, CSK."

There was a pause. No one had bid. RCB signaled they were out. I was happy to be going to CSK as I had thought that if the Indian captain noticed me, I would have a better chance to make it to the Indian team. John asked everyone for one last time if there were any bids.

"Sold!" said John as he slammed the gavel.

CSK were a happy lot. There were a few handshakes. I was jumping with joy in my drawing room. But just then, KXIP claimed they had raised the baton before the gavel in John's hand went down. There was a halt in the proceedings. John was hesitant to disallow Punjab as he hadn't seen them raising the baton, but the Punjab management was quite determined. Unfortunately, there were no third umpires here! John had to make a decision quickly. He checked with the other teams but no one had seen Ashlesha raise the baton as she was sitting at the corner table. After constant persistence from KXIP's side, John allowed them to join the bid again. The CSK were furious with the decision but john convinced them and the auction continued.

"Two hundred and eighty, KXIP."

Immediately, CSK raised it.

"Three hundred lakhs, Punjab."

"Three hundred and twenty, CSK." It looked like the CSK wanted me real bad.

"Three hundred and fifty, KXIP." Ashlesha was going hand in hand with CSK. The moment CSK made a bid; she would raise it the very next second.

"Do I have three hundred and eighty?" John asked.

And this time, it was CSK who signaled they were out. John waited for a few seconds and slammed the gavel, only this time looking at the bidders and not down.

"*Sold!*"

That was it. The moment was sealed. I had created history. No uncapped player had been sold for such a price before. I had become the most expensive uncapped player in the history of the IPL. Ashlesha and other members of the KXIP looked really happy with the buy as one could see the smiles and handshakes.

Meanwhile, I was jumping on the bed with the phone in my hand. I had dialled Bose da to give him an 'I told you so!'

It was a very crucial time for me as far as my career was concerned. The IPL could turn things around for me. This was my opportunity to make it big and turn my dream of playing for India into reality.

The Indian Premiere League or the IPL is a T-20 or twenty over per side cricket tournament. A total of eight teams play the tournament. All the eight teams represent a particular state or city of India. Each team plays all the seven opponents twice and the top four teams move on to the next stage, which is the qualifiers. The teams get eliminated one by one until the final and the winner is then decided by a match between the best two teams.

The IPL was nearing and I was requested to report in Mohali, Punjab a week before our first match. I reported positive for my availability and reached Mohali on the given date. A person from the management received me at the airport and helped me to check-in at the hotel. The owners had organized a dinner in the evening for the players so that the new entrants could get comfortable with the old ones and get rid of any sort of diffidence they had. All this was pretty new and big for me. I was feeling like a small kid in a carnival who looks at every toy shop and every ride with fascination in his eyes. There were so many of my heroes dining together – Virender Sehwag, Glenn

Maxwell, the Coach Sanjay Bangar amongst others and here I was, shaking hands with them and having a casual conversation with them. All the stuff that I had only dreamt of till date. To my surprise, all of them were very warm and welcomed me and a couple of other uncapped players with smiles and hugs. There were also a few international players who had joined our team, but they seemed to know the existing players quite well already. While all this was going on, I spotted someone in a black gown with her hair tied up in a bun. It was Ashlesha and she looked ravishing. She had a constant smile on her face; it was really charming. I had never seen someone so bubbly and full of life.

"Hey there, Suhaan Arora, right? I am Ashlesha Kapoor," she said putting forward her hand after confirming my identity and introducing herself – a common level of stupidity all girls possess. I mean, she had spent crores on me so she had to know me. Moreover, she was the one who was paying me so much and I'd be a fool if I didn't know who she was.

"Yes, that's me, and you certainly don't need to introduce yourself. Big fan!" I said after a firm handshake and gave her a big smile.

"We are really counting on you to perform well this season. We have all seen your Ranji performance and we truly wish that you continue the same form here," she said.

"Trust me, the price tag has put me under a lot of pressure and I am going to give it my best shot to justify that," I said.

"You have a beautiful smile," I thought of saying but stopped just before it was ready to come out of my mouth. You just cannot flirt with your employer in the first meeting!

"Okay then, see you around. All the best!" she said and moved on to meet other people while I roamed about alone, staring at one face after another with a drink in my hand.

From the next morning, the uncapped players started practicing with a few local boys and a day later, the international players also joined us. Fortunately for me, the coach and captain George Bailey were happy with the line and length I was bowling and they had already told me that I'd be playing the first game ahead of Anureet Singh, their regular seam bowling option. They said they were giving me a chance because it'd be the start of the tournament. Another reason was that the match was going to be played in Ahmedabad where I had played a lot of cricket. My batting abilities could prove to be handy as well.

Our first match was against Rajasthan Royals at the Sardar Patel Stadium, Motera, Ahmedabad. We had flown in after practicing in Mohali, just a day before the match.

"They have a strong batting line-up with a great mix of international and local players. With the likes of Australian power hitters like Shane Watson, James Faulkner and Steve Smith, I know they can pack a punch; and with Rahane and Sanju Samson, they look like a formidable batting line-up. We'll have to bowl really well to win this one," Bailey said at the team meeting just a few hours before the match.

After the team meeting, we headed to the ground to warm up a bit and what I saw there was fantastic. It was about 7:15 p.m. and the ground was filling up with spectators. It was a human sea out there cheering for their favourite players and team. I had watched quite a few matches before on this ground but the feeling of being on the other side was something else. The Ranji matches which we played here hardly had any spectators. The lights, the setup, the cameras at all angles, and the security made it seem like a different place altogether. After much difficulty, I put all those emotions aside and concentrated on the match. It was my first big game where thousands were going to watch me. Performing well was a compulsion for me and not an option.

"*Kem chho* Ahmedabad!" Ravi Shastri began the toss proceedings in his usual affectionate fashion. George Bailey and Steve Smith were standing in the middle with him.

Two Australian players captaining two sides in an Indian League – such was the beauty of the IPL where arch rivals turned friends in a matter of days, and players who represent the same country fought it out with one another for glory.

"Rajasthan Royals have won the toss and elected to bat first," Ravi announced as Bailey signalled that we are bowling first. Soon, we got back to the dressing room and changed into our attires.

The normal cricket pant and shirt which was the first uniform of cricketers had changed considerably along with the evolution of the game. For starters, the pants had changed into tracks and shirts into t-shirts. Moreover, technology had given rise to heat resistant t-shirts, t-shirts made from recycled wastes and so on. The major change apart from this was the amount of logos the t-shirts carried. The situation is such that you can hardly find any more spots to put an advertisement for your product. Players look more like advertisement boards than human beings.

"Okay guys, so this is where it all begins. Winning the first match is the most important step in such a long series. If we start on a positive note, we get more inclined to carry that same momentum into the coming games. So let's go out there and give this crowd one heck of a game!" Bailey motivated all of us just before the game started. We were all standing in a huddle and listening to him carefully.

Sandeep Sharma, the right arm bowler was asked to open the bowling. Bailey told me I'd be bowling the next one. Sandeep bowled a nice over with nice swing and conceded only four runs. It was my turn now and I was raring to go.

"The tougher the opponent, the more glory you'll achieve when you defeat him," I said to myself, while taking the ball in my hands and marking my run-up. I got ready to bowl to Shane Watson, one of the most destructive batsmen in the world.

I ran in and bowled him a fast, in-swinging yorker.

"Howzzat!" I appealed to the umpire. Watson had missed the ball which stuck him on his pads. Luckily for him, the ball was missing the leg stump and the umpire signalled he was not out.

"Whoa! This lad bowls with some serious pace. The last ball was 145.2 kph!" Ravi said on the mike from the commentary box.

Next up, I had made up my mind to bowl him an out-swinger like I always do. I did, but Watson read it and let it pass to the keeper.

Next, I decided to bowl an in-swinger again, but at a fuller length.

"Howzzat!" I appealed loudly and the wicket-keeper and the slip fielders appealed with me. To my extreme delight, the umpire raised his finger and I just had my first wicket. I had got the start that I wanted. I wanted to make a mark and I was happy I had managed to do that.

"Well, he can bowl the in-swinger, the out-swinger and has got tremendous pace. I must say I am very impressed and will be keeping an eye on him," Ravi said.

The evening continued to delight me because by the end of the Rajasthan Royals innings, I had picked up 3 wickets and had given away only 14 runs in my 4 overs. Also, we had managed to bowl them out for only 113 runs. We won the match with ease as Virender Sehwag and the middle order batsman Wriddhiman Saha chased it down and I was adjudged the Man of the Match.

"The first one amongst the many more to come," I thought and collected it.

"You were steaming in there tonight young man, congratulations. After such a complete performance, what are the areas you think you can work on?" Simon Doull, the former cricketer and presenter asked me.

"Well, I think it's too early to get too greedy and think ahead of what is required. Yes, I am very happy with my performance and would like to continue the same way, but I have to admit the pitch was helping the bowlers early on and we exploited it pretty well."

"You were bowling at around 145 kph regularly and I feel the Indian team needs fast bowlers direly. You think you could be an answer to the problem?"

"I'd surely love to be! But again, it has been only one match and I don't want to think too far ahead," I replied trying to sound as modest as I could.

"All the best for the coming games."

"Thanks, cheers," I said and left for the dressing room.

Everybody was happy with my performance and I couldn't have asked for anything more. I needed to seal my place in the team and it was a great start towards that goal. Ashlesha, who was watching the match from the VIP box was also ecstatic when she came down and congratulated me and the rest of the team.

Next, we were up against the CSK, the most consistent team in the history of the IPL by far. To win this, we had to do our very best. There was something about the IPL and MS Dhoni. He was anyway a great captain and a champion batsman, but when it came to IPL, his plans and their execution seemed to be at another level. Many a time, a cricket fan had witnessed targets of over 200 runs being chased down effortlessly and targets under 140 being defended by the CSK, with much credit going to Dhoni. The match was to be played in Mohali, our home ground. We had won the toss this time and were fielding first. It was a huge mountain to climb in the first step itself because they had the most devastating opening pair of all teams – New Zealand captain Brendon McCullum and West Indian power hitter Dwayne Smith.

As expected, they started off the innings in attack mode and scored 12 runs off Sandeep's over. It was my turn next and I had made up my mind I'd not get intimidated by these big names. But I should have known, they were not big names for nothing. Brendon McCullum clobbered me all around the park for 18 runs in my over. Before the ball could swing or do something, he would step out and hit it to any area which he wished to. He had hit me for three sixes in my first four deliveries and after the fourth one I was feeling helpless. I somehow completed the over without giving any more runs.

"Welcome to the real cricketing world, Mr Suhaan Arora!" I said to myself as I ran towards the third man to take my fielding position. Even a five-year-old-kid could spot my chagrined face.

Their score was 30/0 after two overs and Sandeep's third over brought no good news for us as the score had already reached 45/0. Captain Bailey trusted me with one more over and asked me to stick to the basics even if I went for runs. His confidence in me gave me a thumbs up and I got ready to bowl with much more determination.

I ran in and bowled a short delivery aimed right at around his chest so that he didn't get room to swing his bat freely. As I had thought, he stepped out and got beaten.

"I want the third man a bit finer, a deep point and a long on," I told Bailey. In a twenty over match, only three fielders are allowed outside the thirty yard circle for the first six overs. I had placed all of them on the off-side to make the batsman think what I was trying to do. According to the field, I should have bowled only outside the off stump, but I bowled a short delivery aimed at his chest again. This time, he didn't advance forward and just defended it. I was getting successful in making him think. The next delivery, the third one of my second over, I bowled just a bit short out-swinger as I thought he would advance once again and swing his bat.

"Catch it!"

We all shouted in unison as the ball was travelling towards the third man. He obliged, and we had our first wicket. The plan had worked. McCullum had advanced forward and edged the ball and it went flying to third man because of the speed.

The team was suddenly instilled with a new confidence and we were looking like a different team after that wicket. We got all charged up and bowled well for the entire innings and restricted them to 154 runs. We won this match as well with ease as the batting department was going strong. Once again, I had a good day on the field as I ended up with four wickets this time.

"You were quite impressive today," Ashlesha said. I was sitting by the swimming pool of the hotel as I couldn't sleep.

"Thanks. What are you doing here? It's quite late, shouldn't you be sleeping?" I asked.

"I can ask you the same question!" she replied.

"Hehe, yeah I should be, but couldn't."

"Great! I think we can talk a bit to kill some time," she said.

"Sure, most welcome."

"So tell me something about Suhaan Arora," she said and we started talking.

Talking to her was more like me listening and she speaking, but still some could argue it was a dialogue and not a monologue. It seemed like talking was her ambition in life and she was on a mission to blabber at least a billion sentences before she dies. No wonder she could talk to someone like me who she didn't know at all for hours. I told her the reason why I couldn't sleep was Namrata. I told her everything about Namrata and she was apologetic and had tears in her eyes. It was quite surprising how well she handled the team management when in reality she was just a kid. Her explanation to my query was she loved cricket more than movies and watched every match. It was because of her constant pestering that her father had bought a stake in the team. It was 5.45 in the morning when we realized we had talked through the entire night. We really enjoyed each other's company and went to our respective rooms after we promised to do it again if we were sleep deprived in future.

The tournament progressed and so did our good run. We ran past one opponent after the other and continued to win matches comprehensively, barring a few hiccups. By the end of the league stage, we had won 10 out of our 14 matches and were sitting comfortably on top of the table. Meanwhile, the purlieus of the hotel's swimming pool in Mohali had become mine and Ashlesha's hangout place. As we were supposed to play 7 out of our 14 league matches in Mohali, we had got a lot of evenings to get to know each other. Then, it was time for the playoffs.

We were supposed to face KKR as they were placed second just behind us. The winner of the match would book a place in the finals and hence we were craving for the win. Though we had defeated them on both the occasions in the league stages, we had to be wary that they were very close contests and we had won only by 3 runs, coincidentally on both occasions. We had won the toss. They had won the tosses previously and had asked us to bat first both the times. This time, Bailey won the toss and selected to bat as we thought it was an important game and a good score on the board would put them under pressure. Interestingly, it seemed like KKR had their plans chalked out pretty nicely as well as they were playing four spinners, thinking that our power hitters were all foreign players who are generally uncomfortable against spin. Three of their spinners were foreign players, including the mystery man Sunil Naraine and the fourth one was Piyush Chawla, the leg spinner.

The match started and very soon, it looked like their plan had worked to perfection because at the end of six overs or the powerplay, we were 5 wickets down for just 23 runs. After that debacle though, there was some respite as Bailey and David Miller steadied the innings and took the score to 90/5 after 15 overs.

"Catch it!" the KKR fielders shouted as the ball went high in the air and the keeper settled under it after Miller had mis-hit a delivery from Sunil Naraine. The keeper took a simple catch and Miller was out. Meanwhile, the batsmen had crossed and Bailey was on strike.

"Oh, he's cleaned him up! What a delivery to get George Bailey out. This is a very crucial wicket and the KXIP are down in the tatters!" the commentator said.

The score was 90/7 after 15.2 and for the first time in this tournament, I walked out to bat as we had never lost more than 6 wickets in the entire series.

"We have to get to 120 at least so that we get something to bowl at. So play carefully and take singles and doubles. We still have almost 5 overs," Mitchell Johnson or MoJo, the Australian fast bowler and my companion at the other end advised me as

I was getting ready to face Naraine. I, on the other hand, had other plans.

"He has got a couple of hundreds in the Ranji as well, this young southpaw, which says he can bat. Oh, he has danced down the track and hit it hard and the ball is travelling and it's a six!" Sunil Gavaskar said from the commentary box.

I knew it would be very difficult to understand which way Naraine's ball would spin, so I decided to hop down the track, make it a full-toss and hit it powerfully.

"Oh he has come down the track again and hit Naraine for another six! This is entertaining," Sunil continued.

I defended the next delivery somehow and managed to take a single off his last ball. The score was 103/7 after 16 overs.

Bradd Hogg was supposed to bowl the next over. I had been studying him on TV during the entire innings and I could sense what area he is going to bowl. I swept him thrice in the over for one six and two boundaries and once again picked up a single off the last ball. Mitchell, my partner was happy to give me the strike. The score was now 118/7 after 17 overs.

Next up, it was the Indian fast bowler Umesh Yadav. Playing a fast bowler and hitting him around the park had become my forte during the club and Ranji days and I tried to do the same here. I thought we had expected to get around 120 after 20 overs, but we were here 3 overs earlier, and hence I would swing my bat at anything and everything. Once again, the strategy worked for me as I managed to hit two balls out for six and stole 12 runs from the over.

Mitchell hit the first delivery of the 19th over from Piyush Chawla to long on for a single and gave me the strike. Piyush bowled a few quicker ones and gave away only 5 runs in the over. Andre Russell bowled the last over and gave away ten runs. I hit nine of them and in the process completed my 50. Our final score was 145/7. We were quite happy with the score as it could have been much worse. The Kolkata batting line-up was no match for our bowling that night as Johnson and I hunted in a pair and picked up 5 wickets between us and got them all out for 126 runs, booking our berth in the final.

"I didn't get a chance in the entire series to bat and prove myself, but I am glad I could do it today. I would surely like to bat up the order like one or two down, but my primary role is that of a bowler so I am happy with whatever the captain has in mind for me," I said at the post-match presentation.

"Well played young man. It was mesmerizing. If you continue this way, I am sure you will go a long way," Ravi Shastri said as we were moving out of the stadium to get back to our hotel. I was being applauded and praised by one and all, but a compliment from the veteran was huge.

The next morning, I was reading the *Times of India* and there was a big photo of mine on the front page.

'KXIP Reach the Final, Courtesy Suhaan Arora' it read. I had featured on the sports page before this for my consistent bowling performance, but featuring on the headlines of the highest selling newspaper in the country was splendid. We were supposed to catch a flight to Kolkata to play the final at the Eden Gardens. As we were moving out of the hotel to get into the team bus, I saw a few pretty girls hurrying towards me.

"Hello Suhaan, we are big fans. Can we take a selfie with you please?"One of the girls asked. This was new for me and I didn't know how to react as I was surprised. I agreed after Murli Vijay signalled me. All of a sudden I felt like a star. I obliged them with ten photos instead of one and could have agreed for a few more but they had to leave. There were a few camera persons clicking my photos and I loved it all. We had a four day break before the final game and apart from practicing, I gave a couple of interviews to leading channels and newspapers. I was soaking in all the admiration from a few fans which I had made.

Finally, the D-day arrived and we were up against the most star-studded side in the IPL – the Mumbai Indians. Think of all the best players of all the three departments – batting, bowling, fielding – they had them on their side. Their fielding coaches were Robin Singh and Jhonty Rhodes – the best in the world. Their bowling coach was Shane Bond, considered as one of the best New Zealand has ever produced and then, it was the batting department with two of the best batsman the game has and will ever produce – Sachin Ramesh Tendulkar and Ricky Ponting. If this was not enough, their playing eleven included the best T-20 players – Lasith Malinga, Keiron Pollard, and Rohit Sharma amongst others. We had lost only three games out of our 14, with one being abandoned due to rain, and one of those three teams to beat us was MI. The one which we had won against them was at a time when they were playing their worst cricket and had already lost their first three matches. But since then, they had shuffled their squad a bit and the inclusion of a few new foreign faces had done wonders for them. Everybody saw a mercurial rise in the way they played which was reflected in their 8 wins out of the played 10 games.

For the team meeting, all of us, including the support staff, assembled in the centre of the Eden Gardens at 8 in the morning.

"As we all know, Mumbai are playing tremendously well at this point of time and we'll have to be at our very best to defeat them. It's going to be a tough nut to crack and the sooner we realize that and be prepared mentally, the better it'll be for us," Coach Sanjay Bangar said.

"There has been some amount of dew by late evening every day since we have arrived here and the ball will not grip. The spinners will face difficulty to spin the ball and also batting will become a bit easy and so, we must field first if we win the toss," he continued after a few more things were discussed and Bailey and a couple of senior players agreed with him.

"Sir, I think it's a big game and batting second could put us under a lot of pressure. You yourself just said that Mumbai is going to come hard at us, and a couple of wickets down early on while chasing will put us under a lot of pressure," I interrupted.

"See, we cannot ignore the dew factor. It'll make a difference of at least 15-20 runs and that's a big chunk to let go," he explained.

"Sir, I think the mind factor will play a bigger role than the dew thing. If they happen to score anything above 165, we'll be mentally under pressure from ball one. Secondly, with the kind of batting line-up we have, scoring 70-75 runs in the last five or six overs won't seem like such a big task as compared to doing the same thing while chasing. Lastly, Mumbai always likes to bat first. They are very bad at chasing and that'll be a big boost for us," I said.

"I think he has a point," Viru Paaji said.

"Me too," Maxi followed, and then Bailey. Finally, Bangar also agreed.

It seemed as if the gods were smiling upon us as we won the toss and chose to bat first. I was a bit nervous now, because if the plan failed, the onus would be on me.

"I would have batted first as well. We feel more comfortable defending totals rather than chasing them," Rohit told the presenter after losing the toss. Bangar gave me a 'thumbs up' after listening to that.

"Hey, Suhaan!"

A voice called out when I was packing my kit near the pitch to go to the team dug-out, and trust me I had never been this surprised ever before. Neither Namrata nor any other person had managed to surprise me this way. It was Mr Sachin Tendulkar – the reason why I, like millions of other aspiring cricketers, had started playing cricket. I had seen him in MI's dug-out on both the previous occasions when we were playing, but had never got a chance to talk to him.

"Err, yes sir?" I replied, thinking why would he call me. What could he possibly talk about with a novice like me?

"I've been following your game since a few matches and I am pretty impressed," the great one said.

"Wow, thank you sir. It means the world to me. Thank you," I replied excitedly.

Here I was, standing in the middle of one of the biggest grounds in the world with the greatest batsman in the world, and he was praising my bowling.

"You are bowling with a pretty good speed, don't ever let that go away," he advised.

"Also, I think if you could work on your batting a bit more, you could prove to be a perfect fast bowling all-rounder our team has been needing for a while," he added.

I was jumping with joy, in my mind that is. What did he mean by 'our team'? Was he talking about the Mumbai Indians? Was he talking about the Mumbai Ranji team? Or was it the Indian team?

"Surely sir, thank you sir," I replied. He also gave me some useful tips on how I could improve my batting. We parted as the game was about to begin.

"That was a pretty long chat Sachin had with Suhaan Arora there," Danny Morrison said in his unusual style.

"Maybe Sachin was giving him some batting tips. I could see him taking a couple of stances and explaining something to the youngster," Sunil Gavaskar said.

I was happy beyond words and wanted to share it with somebody. I don't know why, but I hopped towards the dressing room in search of my phone and dialled Namrata's number. But as soon as I did, I cancelled it. I don't know what had made me do that. Was she still such an inseparable part of me, at least subconsciously? May be it was a big thing for me and I wanted her to be the first to know. Thankfully, it hadn't started ringing.

Viru Paaji and Vijay had started off our innings in a blistering fashion and taken the score to 36/0 after just 3 overs. They were particularly harsh on Malinga, extracting 30 runs from his 2 overs. Mitchell McClenaghan, the New Zealand fast bowler ran in to bowl his second over.

"Ooohhh!" the fielders reacted as the first ball missed the stumps by a whisker. Murli Vijay was the batsman.

"Howzzat!" a loud appeal for LBW was ruled in favour of the batsman on the second delivery.

"Bowled him!"

This time, McClenaghan had his man. He was troubling Vijay since the first ball and was finally rewarded.

"Glenn Maxwell is the next man in. It has been an on and off season for him, but he has hit a couple of crucial knocks for Punjab and they'd be really counting on him to perform well."

Bailey was in an aggressive mode as he had instructed Maxi to attack the bowlers straight away.

"Pad up Suhaan, you're next," Bailey said patting on my shoulder.

"Huh, me?" I asked surprised.

"Yep, you'll be going in next as a pinch hitter. Go after their bowling, swing your bat hard and make as many runs as you can and as fast as you can. If it works, well and good; if it doesn't, it'll be worth a shot."

Pinch hitters was a concept which had become more popular with the rise of T-20 cricket and I padded up thinking Bailey was right in trying to implement it here as we still had 4 batsmen after me who could stabilize the innings if the plan didn't work.

"Bowled him!" It was Viru Paaji now. It was the last ball of the fourth over and McClenaghan had produced another beauty to get rid of him. The score was 37/2 after 4 overs and I joined Maxi at the center.

"Well well well, we are in for a surprise here. Suhaan Arora has walked out in the middle instead of David Miller. He did take the KKR bowlers to the cleaners the other night but this could backfire if he ends up wasting too many deliveries because Punjab really needs to put up a big score on the board."

Nobody, not me, not the Mumbai Indians, and not even Bailey would have thought his plan would work out the way it did. Maxi and I battered the MI bowlers to all parts of the ground for the next sixteen overs. Maxi hit all his exclusive reverse sweeps, slog hits over mid-wicket region and I targeted the long-on and long-off regions. The paucity of quality in their bowling was thoroughly exploited by us. Maxi had scored a brilliant 108 runs from just 57 deliveries and I took 39 deliveries for my score of 67. By the end of the 20th over, we hadn't lost another wicket and after adding a few extras, our score was 223/2.

"It was one such day when the fielders had become spectators and the spectators had become fielders," Harsha Bhogle spoke into the mike.

Defending this kind of a total in such a pressure game was just a formality and we bundled our opposition out for just 123 runs. We were the new champions. The dug-out was ecstatic. There were fireworks all around. Ashlesha came and gave me a long bear hug. When she released her grip and we came face to face, I don't know why but I was not that happy to see her face. Perhaps I was retrogressing as I was expecting it to be Namrata's. But I let such feelings go and hugged her again. We all jumped and danced in joy after forming a huddle.

"Hey, what are you doing here all alone?" Ashlesha asked me from behind. She was standing at the terrace gate while I was leaning on the side wall of the terrace of the hotel in Mumbai where the team was celebrating our IPL triumph the very next evening.

The party was going on downstairs and I was in no mood to be there. There was a long list of celebrities, from the hottest chicks and movie stars whom I had only seen on the screen to the wives and girlfriends of cricketers, a few big shot businessmen too, but nothing interested me. In fact, I felt like I needed a break from this entire world to search for my quantum of solace so that I could confide in it for a while and come back afresh.

"Hey, nothing, just felt like I could miss the noise for some time. How did you know I'd be here?" I turned and replied. She was looking steaming hot in a shiny silver dress which was quite short and was also revealing a bit of her cleavage. She was holding a drink in one hand and the door handle with the other. This, I thought could be an exception from all the things which were failing to get my attention the entire evening.

"The swimming pool in this hotel is on the terrace, that's how. The DJ is on fire down there. You should come and have some fun," she said while she came and stood next to me and moved her fingers near my neck in a seductive way.

"Thank you for the offer, but I think I'll pass," I said removing her hand. She was a bit drunk, but not so much that she didn't realize what she was doing.

"Oh come on, don't tell me you don't feel attracted towards me," she said, and leaned towards me and kissed me.

"I am sorry, I don't think I can do this," I said pulling myself away after a couple of seconds.

"No, I am sorry, I don't know what I was doing," she said and after a few awkward seconds, she turned and began to walk towards the terrace gate.

Just then, I stopped her by putting my hand on her shoulder and turned her around. Our eyes met for a second and I could sense getting lost in hers. I grabbed her dress and pulled her towards me, kissing her hard. She kissed me back. I could feel the softness of her lips as I could feel every inch of her delicate body pressed against mine.

"Now for some sports news, the Test squad for India's tour to England in the coming month has been announced. Here is the list of players included: MS Dhoni will lead the side. Apart from the regular core of Shikhar Dhawan, Virat Kohli, Cheteshwar Pujara, R Ashwin, Bhuvaneshwar Kumar and Mohommad Shami, Ajinkya Rahane and Rohit Sharma have been included in the batting department and Suhaan Arora, the top wicket taker in the Ranji this season and Stuart Binny have been included," the news reporter read out.

"Congratulations! I just saw it on the news. Let's meet up and celebrate," an excited Ashlesha said on the phone. She was calling from Mumbai and I was in Ahmedabad, but she spoke as though we live a couple of blocks away from each other.

"Thank you. Yeah, sure," I said.

"You don't seem that happy. Did you not want this?" she asked.

"No, it's not like that. I kind of knew I was going to make it." I boasted. Bose da had already come home to give me the news before I could possibly get it from any other source.

Soon, I was on the flight to England with the team. We had left three weeks before our first match in order to get accustomed to the conditions there. Owing to my good performances in the practice matches, I was given a chance in the first match.

"What is this, Suhaan? Can I check it out?" Ashlesha asked while I was shaving in the bathroom. She had travelled all the way to England to support me during the third match at the Lord's Cricket Ground in London.

"Yeah sure, just some random videos from college," I said after I saw she was fiddling with my laptop.

"Oh my God! Suhaan, it's just brilliant. I didn't know you could act so well," she was watching a recording of the college play in which I had acted.

"You call that good acting? You definitely don't have high standards in that field for sure then," I said while I jumped in the bed and snuggled up with her and put the laptop aside to make love to her.

The England tour was becoming a sort of a success story for us. After four matches, both sides had won one test match each and the fifth one had become a decider. We were quite pumped up and really wanted to win this one as it would help in erasing our team's image of being lions at home but lambs abroad. After five days of brilliant cricket by the team, we emerged victorious and managed to win the series by a 2-1 margin. My bowling and batting were appreciated by one and all and I couldn't ask for anything more. Ashlesha seemed to be happier than me after the win. She had joined the team celebration with the wives and girlfriends of a few other players and was absolutely ecstatic about my performance. God couldn't be more kind, I thought.

The next morning, we thought of travelling to London and exploring the city as I had never been there before. The ODI series was supposed to begin after a gap of around two weeks and we had some time to relax.

"Suhaan, Dad wants to talk to you," Ash said handing over her phone to me. We were on one of the open roof top buses which are used for city tours.

"What? Why?" I asked shocked.

"Just talk to him and you'll know, baba," she whispered and signalled me to talk.

"Hello sir, how are you?" I asked, just about managing to start off what I thought would be a very awkward conversation.

"Hey, I am good. I have been watching your performance, great going, son," he replied.

"Thank you, sir."

"But I'd like to mention that I have seen one more performance of yours which has impressed me a lot as well," he said.

"Err, I didn't quite get you. Which performance, sir?" I asked. What was he talking about? Which performance had impressed him so much? And why was he calling and telling me about it? What was going on?

"Well, it seems you do not know that Ash had sent me the video of that college play of yours a couple of days ago and I think you were great in it."

"What!" I gave Ash a stern look. Why would she do that?

"Yes, and after seeing that I think I have a role for you in my next movie which I am making with Ashlesha."

"*What!* You can't be serious. Is this a joke, Ash? What is going on here?" I asked her while I was still on the phone. Meanwhile, she was grinning continuously.

"Yes, son, it's not a joke. I have sent the details to Ash. Do think about it and let me know. Have a good day," he said and disconnected.

I was completely bewildered. This was by far the strangest call of my life. I, of all people in the world had been offered a movie. How does one react in a situation like this? How can it be so casual? My mind was not able to process it for a good few minutes until Ashlesha spoke and explained everything to me. She had seen the video the other day and liked it instantly. Meanwhile, she was now two movies old and her dad wanted to work with her and was working on a script since a couple of months. They were about to begin hunting for the lead actor and it was then that she had posted the video to him. Quite surprisingly, he had also liked it and they thought there was enough hype in the media and amongst the people about my affair with Ashlesha and they could benefit from that.

"Great. But it's not that easy, madam. My career has just started shaping up. I just played my first series and I intend to play many more. How is it even possible? Do you guys want me to quit playing cricket? You and your father must be crazy to even think about anything like that."

"No silly, we are not suggesting anything like that. My father makes movies for the masses which are filled with Bollywood masala. This movie is also a remake of a super-hit South Indian romantic-comedy, so the entire shooting will be in Mumbai itself and may be a couple of foreign locations for a song or a few scenes. We can complete the entire shooting in two months flat, which is when you are not playing against anyone."

"I don't know, Ash. All this is so sudden. I need to think," I said, still blank.

"See, our relationship has become a hot topic for the youngsters and the media these days. Moreover, even you have become immensely popular in such a short span of time. I think it's a great idea, but still it's your decision. Nobody is forcing you, but I'll be glad if you say yes. Think about it and let me know in a day or two," she persuaded me.

We roamed about on the streets of London for the next couple of days apart from visiting the famous places. I had not been able to decide whether to say yes to the offer or not.

"You've always wanted to be famous; this could take it to another level. It's just one movie; you don't have to commit to any more if you don't like the experience. But what if people don't like me? What if I don't act well? What if people start making fun of me? In India, becoming a hero takes ages but a zero is launched every other minute." I was talking to myself while standing under the shower. I had returned to Ahmedabad.

"Hey there, Mr Popular, how are you? I have been watching you play bro, big fan. In fact Mehr has a big crush on you now. She had never watched a game until you started playing and now she doesn't miss even one of them," Akshay said on the phone.

"Haha! Thank you so much. That means a lot to me. Okay listen, I have called you for your advice about something important."

And then, I narrated the entire situation to him and asked him whether I should go for it or not. I then called up Saurabh, Raju, Sanjana, Kanika and each one of my friends for their feedback.

"Definitely bro, that's a great idea. Go for it!" Akshay had said. Mehr had gone to the extent of promising me to watch it twice already.

"Do add a couple of kissing scenes or else I am not going!" Raju said, who was still a virgin.

"You should certainly give it a shot! You were great in that college play and I am pretty sure you and Ashlesha Kapoor will make a great pair," Kanika said on Skype. She had become even hotter. But the most valuable advice came from my most valuable friend, Saurabh.

"Bro, you can go for it, but don't compromise with cricket for it. That is your first love; you left Namrata for it, remember? And secondly, even if the movie fails, you can always play good cricket and win people's love back," he said. It was his and my parents' support, which gave me the confidence to agree to do the movie.

It seemed like Mr Kapoor and his team were waiting to sign the lead actor and get on with the project immediately. Principal photography for the film began as soon as I came on board and the film was ready to be shot in no time. As far as cricket was concerned, I was on a break as we were supposed to play Australia in Australia after a long gap of about four months.

"Cut! Good shot, Suhaan. Take a break everyone!" the director said giving me a thumbs up after I spoke my line correctly. It was the *mahurat* or the first shot of the film and they had chosen to shoot it with me and Ash. Luckily, we managed to pull it off in the first take itself. This was much easier than performing in front of a live audience, because here, you could make as many mistakes as you wanted and still go for another take. Also, playing cricket in front of a large number of spectators had helped me to a certain extent and had given me the much needed confidence.

I'll try and give every scene my best shot and it's up to the audience then to like me or not, I thought. The shooting began and the entire unit was really supportive towards me so that I get adjusted to the setup easily. From the spot boy to the make-up dadas, from Ash to the assistant directors; everybody liked me and I liked them too. Everything was going on nicely until that terrible day – the day when the director came and told me we were supposed to shoot for a dance sequence next.

"It will be shot in the rain. It's a romantic song where you two have just fallen in love with each other and are expressing your feelings," the director said.

"Oh God, please don't make me do that. The thought of doing something like that is already getting me all embarrassed," I explained my hesitation.

"It's a lovely song. Imran has written the most beautiful lines ever and Shiva-Kripa duo has composed it equally well. Don't worry, you'll love it," he said trying to give me some confidence.

"I don't know man. Watching the actors on screen seems like it is very natural and easy for them, but now that I am in their shoes, I know what they go through," I said to Ashlesha after rehearsing the first few lines. It was indeed very difficult. Most of the times I couldn't control my laughter, and the times when I managed to, Ash would burst out seeing me making those romantic faces.

After a couple of nightmarish days, we finally managed to finish off the song and it came out really well. I have to admit the entire credit would be the director's for making me look good. He had managed to make me look like a chocolate boy when the truth is I was nowhere close to anything like that. As Ash had promised, we did manage to complete the entire shooting in about two months. Everybody was really positive about how the shooting had fared and was hopeful of the movie being liked by the people.

"The Tamil version was a super-hit, Dad, and so will this be. Relax," Ash told her dad. We were at their place. The shooting was completed and only the editing and promotion bit was left.

"The Tamil version had the superstar Dhanush in it. They had to love it. You can't be sure if people will accept Suhaan or not," Mr Kapoor said.

"They will, Dad. They like him as a cricketer and hence they surely will accept him. You weren't one bit nervous when you signed him, so why the jitters now?"

"I am still confident, beta. It's just that I am really hopeful about this particular movie. I want it to be a big hit. The thing is, my last few movies haven't done that well. In fact, I have incurred losses for two straight years now and that too huge ones. Also, I lost huge sums of money in planning to start a channel of my own which didn't work out. Thankfully, I pulled out of it before I could lose everything, but still there are losses to cover and it will be a big blow to me if this movie also goes the same way," he said. Ash was shocked to hear that. Her dad had never told her anything about being in debt.

"Don't worry, Dad, the movie is releasing on Diwali. Even if the movie is not that good, people will go and watch it during the first weekend. You won't have to bear any losses, trust me," she said and hugged him.

We left no stones unturned and promoted the movie the best way we could. We went to every reality show that aired on TV, we went to the serials to make special appearances, we did press conferences, and public performances. We did a few PR stunts as well. We went to temples and mosques with the media to show how we were praying for the movie to do well. All in all, we did everything to make sure the movie goers waited for the movie's release. Finally, it was Diwali time and we all were praying. Only this time, we truly were.

"Suhaan Arora is a breath of fresh air."

—*Hindustan Times*

"All-rounder on the field, and an all-rounder off it."

—*The Times of India*

"Kapoor gives the audience another masala entertainer movie and a new star to the country."

—*DNA*

"Where do they sizzle more, on-screen or in reality?"
—*The Telegraph* quoted with a still of Ash and me.

Ash was reading out the headlines from the entertainment pages of all the leading newspapers. The movie was receiving a great response. It was being loved by everyone. The critics were also generous in rating it. Mr Kapoor's experiment of pairing Ashlesha and me as an on-screen couple had worked big time, and he was finally a happy man. The movie got a big opening and raked in big sums during the entire week following Diwali. People were loving the entertainer. The guys had fallen in love with Ash one more time and I was getting all the female attention.

"It has been shot in Mumbai and South Africa and the entire shoot was wrapped in fifty-four days flat. Suhaan was a thorough professional and I look forward to working with him again," Mr Kapoor said while getting into his car when the reporters mobbed him after the film's success.

"As long as he performs on the field, we do not care what he does when he is not playing, as long as it's not illegal!" Mr Thakur, the BCCI secretary said when he was interviewed.

"So Suhaan, where do you plan to take yourself from here? People are loving your movie *Being Stupid*. Will you be quitting cricket?" Jaanvi Mehta, the reporter asked me. I had been called to the *Headlines Today* office for an interview with her.

"No, nothing like that is going to happen. Cricket is my first love. *Being Stupid* was madness and it just happened because of Mr Kapoor's strange confidence in me. I am going to continue playing cricket as long as my body permits me to," I answered.

"Well, that's good news for all your cricket fans. But on the other hand, your female fans are dying to know about your next movie. Have you signed any yet?" Jaanvi asked.

"No, not yet, and I might not even do any more movies. As I said, this movie just happened out of nowhere. I am a full time cricketer, so I don't think I'll be able to handle both. This might well be my last movie," I said.

"What are you saying? That can't be. People have welcomed you with open arms. Don't you think you are making a hasty decision?"

"I am not making any decisions, Jaanvi. I am just saying that I think it's very difficult. I loved the experience of *Being Stupid*, and if time and fate permit, I'd surely like to act again."

"Have you ever thought of balancing both by playing only in a single format and quitting the other two or something of that sort?"

"Okay, you surely are toying with me now. I just played my first series for India. How can I think about quitting already?" I answered after getting shocked by her immature questions.

"We have come to know that you are a divorcee. Would you like to share something about that and let your fans get to know you better?" Jaanvi asked.

I chose to skip that question as it had made me very uncomfortable. Suddenly, I missed Namrata again. In all this madness that was going around me, I had always felt a constant emptiness in my heart.

After a few more weird questions, I requested her to end the interview.

From the day the movie released and started making a buzz, I started receiving phone calls. There were many well wishers, friends and family, but a few were also the kind I hadn't expected. They were from the industry's big shot directors and producers who wanted to sign me for their movies. I didn't have a manager like other actors. I rejected all those offers politely without even listening to what they had to offer. I wanted to play cricket and the coming few months were going to be very hectic and very important for shaping up my career.

I got past the glitz and glamour of the Hindi film industry and got back to concentrating on cricket. The toughest time that one could experience on the cricket field was when one has to play against Australia, in Australia.

For the next few months, I continued playing cricket and had become a regular member of the Indian team. I was included in the One-day and T-20 side as well and I was enjoying whatever life was offering me. As a lot of experts say, sometimes international cricket looks like an entirely different sport to newcomers as compared to what they play all their lives. One gets to know about the abundance of talent that the other teams have and how difficult it is to get the better of them. I played one more IPL season as well, but our team lost in the playoff stage.

I ran my right hand around her thighs and moved upwards to reach under her mini dress and although not with much power, groped her perfect butt, held her neck with my left and kissed her. She was opening the buttons of my shirt, each one after two or three attempts.

"Suhaan!" a voice called out my name in shock. It was Ashlesha standing at the hotel room door with the bell boy.

Two years had passed since *Being Stupid* had released and I had finally agreed to do another one, after much insistence from Ash. We were in New Zealand shooting for the same. It was being directed and produced by the Chopras – a set of big shots in the movie industry. Priyanka Mehra, a leading actress was starring in the film besides Ash and me. Ash was supposed to start shooting for her part three weeks later and hence only Priyanka and I were in New Zealand. Being of about the same age and having the same amount of love for drinking, it had given us a few nights to hang out at almost all the bars around Auckland. That night was another one of those nights, but the only difference was we had had a little too much to drink and had lost all sense of judgment.

"Ashlesha!" I and Priyanka murmured after regaining some sense.

She was standing at the door and the look on her face signalled shock, anger, and despair at the same time. She dashed out to the corridor after standing at the door for a few seconds.

"I am sorry, I can't do this anymore," I said sitting next to her. She was sitting on a bench near the lake, sobbing.

"Do what?" she asked after a long pause.

"Cheat you."

"What do you mean? Since when has this been going on?" she asked perplexed.

"It has nothing to do with Priyanka…"

"Then who? There have been other women?" she asked angrily.

"Hear me out. I really like you as a person, and I think you are just great. But the thing is I don't love you, Ash. Whenever I spend time with you, I am almost happy, almost excited, almost cheerful, but for some reason it has always failed to fill the gap between almost happy and happy. And that is no fault of yours. Not being able to justify this state was troubling me all the time until you saw me and Priya together. I was kissing Priya, but was craving for Namrata's lips; I was holding Priya but my heart was longing to be close to Namrata. The truth is, I have never been able to forget her and I don't think I will ever be able to do that," I explained. She was already crying when I found her and listening to this had put her in more pain.

"It took two years for you to realize that, Suhaan, two years?" Ashlesha cried inconsolably.

At that moment, her eyes looked like they were carrying the entire world's pain. I had never seen her this way. She was always one of the most cheerful people I had known. I took her by her arm and hugged her.

We flew back to Mumbai after shooting in the most uncomfortable environment. Life, which was already very difficult, was now shouting from within; sometimes asking to change things and at other times, asking to end it altogether. The fact is I had lost all sense of being happy. I was still going with the flow, but for some reason, God had stopped being kind.

Epilogue

"Son, understand that God had never loved you more than me, your friends, or that person standing there," His Holiness said pointing towards a man standing with his baby in his arms.

"Also, he has not stopped loving you now. His love has always been the same for each one of us. You need to know how He impacts our lives. Whatever we do, if it is right, He lays the stepping stones in that direction to help us move forward. Even if we are wrong, He tries to signal us in his own way to stop us. If we understand it and stop, well and good, but even if we don't, he continues loving us anyway," He said while I listened carefully.

"About your problem, Suhaan, a person cannot have everything in life. I have seen the richest lamenting for love from their families and beggars living together happily with empty stomachs. It is human nature to never be satisfied and that is what makes our lives purposeful. According to me, you have done a great job by making your priorities clear and following what your heart told you. Yes of course, you realized it a bit too late and hurt her, but it was the right choice at that point of time.

What you need to understand is that life will not keep giving you chances all the time. You once chose Namrata over cricket and you failed her, you then chose cricket over her and are standing in front of me as a failed person again. Nothing in this world is good or bad. It is human nature to disregard what one has and crave for what one doesn't. But remember one thing, rare are those people who get true love in life, and you are one of those rare people. You should never hurt those who love you and care for you. You should never let such people go away from you. I hope you understand what I am trying to say," He said while ending the speech with a smile on His face. I smiled back and hugged Him to thank Him for the help.

I rushed towards my car as soon as I was out.

"Gaggal!" I told the driver to take me to the airport. I wanted to catch the next flight to Ahmedabad. I wanted to meet Namrata at that very instant. I wanted her back in my life. Everything was crystal clear to me now. The journey from the monastery to the airport seemed like the longest journey of my life.

"Hello Bindiya, how are you?" I asked the maid at Namrata's home after she opened the door.

"I am good, Suhaan babu," she replied.

"I am here to see Namrata, could you please call her?" I asked.

"She doesn't stay here in anymore. She moved out six months ago."

"Oh, where did she go? Do you have her new address?" I asked Bindiya. Luckily, she had it and passed it on to me. I rushed towards the said address to meet her. It was in the Satellite area in Ahmedabad – one of the posh localities with many skyscrapers. She lived on the twenty-second floor of Gateway Towers.

I pressed the doorbell, eagerly waiting to see her again after so many years.

"Turn the gas off, I'll be back in a second," I heard a voice approaching towards me from the other side of the door. It was Namrata's.

"Suhaan!" she said in shock after finding me at her doorstep. I was beaming from ear to ear when I saw her. Dressed in ankle length white denims and a spaghetti strap long top, she was looking as beautiful as ever. But the most beautiful part was the magalsutra around her neck. A tear rolled down my right eye without my even realising.

"Hi, Namrata," I said and hugged her after staring at her for a good thirty seconds. She hesitantly hugged me back.

"Why are you here, Suhaan? What is the meaning of all this? I am married now," she said rather rudely.

"I can see that and trust me, I can't tell you how happy I am. I thought you would be living out your days just for the sake of living and spending the nights with your face between two pillows, because that's what has happened with me. But I am relieved to see you happy. I sure didn't picture this. I have come here to apologize for all the wrong that I have done. I am sorry. I've hurt you a lot and put you through a lot of trouble. I was a fool to behave the way I did. Losing you was and is going to be the biggest loss of my life, but I am happy for you. I am happy that you have moved on and settled down," I blabbered continuously.

"What option did I have, Suhaan? It seemed like life had no purpose after you left me. I tried to move on, but failed numerous times. Then Karan came into my life and changed things. We both know that I'll never be able to love him the way I loved you, yet he accepted me with open arms, and I can't thank him enough for that," she said picking up a photo frame which had their picture in it.

"Sounds like a great guy," I said.

"I forgave you a long time ago, Suhaan. I cursed you for a long time before I realized that not letting you go out of my mind was the reason I wasn't able to move on. It was Karan who told me to forgive you for whatever you did and move on. And see, here I am. I even watch you play at times now, without getting troubled. So don't worry," she said hugging me goodbye.

I left her apartment and cried like a baby in the elevator. But I was relieved because His Holiness' words were running through my mind. Namrata was happy and that is what I wanted. I was relieved to see her happy. She still loved me as a friend and now I wouldn't have to let her go away from me. I had always thought that either I could have Namrata as my life partner or not have her at all. His Holiness had shown me the path which lay in between these two.

Two years later, a bold headline made news all over the world:

Star cricketer and actor Suhaan Arora marries actress Ashlesha Kapoor in a star-studded wedding.

●●●

You Are The Best Wife

Ajay Pandey

This is a true story of two people with contradictory ideologies who fall in love. This is a story of the author after his beloved wife left him halfway through their journey. This heart-warming tale of a boy and a girl who never gave up on their love in face of adversities, ends on a bittersweet and poignant note as Ajay comes to terms with the biggest lesson life has to offer.

An engineer by degree, Ajay works in the IT field and loves to read and trek. He has immortalized his life story through this book.

ISBN: 978-9382665540; Price: 175/-; Pages: 248; Binding: Paperback.

I Still Think About You

Arpit Vageria

For Aamir, little Dhruv is the best gift life has given him. More than just brothers, they are the beginning and end of their family. After years, struggles and pain are slowly fading away in the face of happier times when suddenly everything is thrown into darkness and pain.

This is a story of love, brotherhood, passion, dedication, pain, and the depths to which a heart can go to win back lost love.

Arpit writes scripts and more for the Indian television industry, and enjoys road trips, singing, and adventure sports.

ISBN: 978-9382665700; Price: 195/-; Pages: 185; Binding: Paperback.

It Doesn't Hurt to be Nice

Amisha Sethi

Kiara is a dynamic, thirty-something girl who has reached great heights professionally, and is the apple of the eye for almost everyone who knows her. But she never took any short cuts.

More than Kiara's story and the wisdom she achieves through the various dramatic and hilarious experiences of her life, this book is a motion picture with you in the lead role, perhaps a 2.0 version of you.

Along with holding top notch positions in leading companies in the past thirteen years, Amisha has also done extensive research in ancient scriptures.

ISBN: 978-9382665489; Price: 175/-; Pages: 144; Binding: Paperback.

A Broken Man

Akash Verma

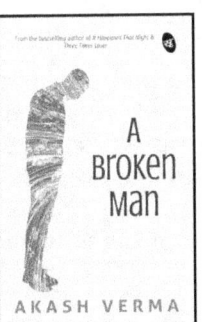

Krishna is a Dalit boy from Bihar who falls in love with Chhavi, a high caste Brahman girl propagating equality in a politically charged Lucknow University campus. Their love is ruthlessly crushed by a society that thrives on divisions of caste and religion.
This book is the quest of a deprived Krishna to redeem hope from despair, love from separation and success out of repeated failures.

Akash Verma is an entrepreneur and has published two bestsellers till now. He is fascinated by cinema, literature, history and travel.

ISBN: 978-9382665694; Price: 195/-; Pages: 240; Binding: Paperback.

When Love Meets Ego

Krishna

Would you dare to fall in love after someone breaks your heart and cheats on you?

What if someone uses you to satisfy their ego? Would you play with someone else's feelings to get even?

When He reaches a new city and encounters people who are already a victim of bruised egos, He finds himself a mere mode or object to satisfy their egos.

Krishna is a software engineer by education and works as lead analyst with a renowned IT giant. He has directed various short films and also acts in commercial ads.

ISBN: 978-9382665670; Price: 175/-; Pages: 160; Binding: Paperback.

Punk Sunk Love

Dhirendra Tiwari

Two men; two personalities; two slants of love; one destiny.

Roy's tender heart is on a quest to find the holy grail of mankind – true love. But, the soft echo of feisty Monica's whispering words will change everything, raining mayhem on him and everyone he touches. His only glimmer of hope is by helping Shammi and swapping his wretchedness with swagger ... the swagger of love.

Dhirendra Tiwari finished his Engineering in Mumbai and Master's in Science from Houston, Texas. He is currently settled in New Jersey with his wife and son.

ISBN: 978-9382665687; Price: 195/-; Pages: 240; Binding: Paperback.